Let's Go to the Park

By

RAYMOND C. MORRISON

Chairman Educational Committee American Institute of Park Executives;
City Forester and Director of the School-Ground Landscaping Program, Fort Worth, Texas

and

MYRTLE E. HUFF

Principal of Columbia School, Elgin, Illinois

Courtesy *Cincinnati Y. M. C. A.*

To

RAYMOND AND PHILIP,

WHOSE LIVES ARE SO INTIMATELY AFFECTED BOTH BY THE GOOD WORKS AND BY THE MISTAKES OF MEN WHO HAVE FASHIONED THEIR ENVIRONMENT, THIS BOOK IS AFFECTIONATELY DEDICATED. TO THEM AND TO MILLIONS OF OTHER BOYS AND GIRLS FALLS THE RESPONSIBILITY OF BUILDING THE CITIES OF TOMORROW. MAY THEY CREATE GARDEN CITIES WHERE THERE WILL BE ABUNDANT FACILITIES FOR RECREATION AND FOR A FULLER, RICHER LIFE FOR ALL.

Foreword

Progress in the realm of industry and business has far outstripped that in Government. Scientific planning and technical development in industry and commerce have made rapid progress, while social science and planning, affecting the fundamental well-being of the people, have lagged far behind.

Today our great problem is one of human engineering. The very permanency of our democratic institutions, of our government itself, rests on our ability to keep our social development in pace with industrial and technical growth.

"A more abundant life for all" requires a healthier and happier environment. It implies more beautiful and pleasant surroundings, with our cities well planned and orderly, serving not only the industrial and commercial needs of the people but satisfying their cultural, aesthetic and recreational desires as well.

Because of improved and expanded means of transportation, closely connecting city with country, it means a countryside in which the natural beauty is conserved or restored, with its rivers clean and unpolluted, its hillsides and uneconomic areas largely wooded.

That all this may be, there must first be the public desire that it shall be. It has been said, "Where there is no light, the people perish." The more enlightenment and understanding on problems growing out of our industrial civilization, which compels people to live and to work together, the better it will be for all.

The hope of the American Institute of Park Executives in sponsoring this book is to create in the minds of all, especially the youth of our land, a love for beauty and an appreciation of the basic problems of building an environment that will contribute to a richer and a happier life for all. Only through an enlightened people can our democracy cope with the problems of the day.

American Institute of Park Executives

OFFICERS

WILLIAM A. STINCHCOMB, Cleveland, Ohio	President
HAROLD S. WAGNER, Akron, Ohio	Vice-President
E. H. BEAN, Brookfield, Illinois	Treasurer
C. P. KEYSER, Portland, Oregon	Past President
WILL O. DOOLITTLE, Tulsa, Oklahoma	Executive Secretary

DIRECTORS.

S. HERBERT HARE,	Kansas City, Missouri
WILLIAM R. READER,	Calgary, Alta., Canada
E. A. GALLUP,	Ann Arbor, Michigan
V. K. BROWN,	Chicago, Illinois
WALTER L. WIRTH,	New Haven, Connecticut

EDUCATIONAL COMMITTEE.

FRANK T. GARTSIDE,	Washington, D. C.
DONALD F. GORDON,	Oklahoma City, Oklahoma
EARL F. ELLIOTT,	Rockford, Illinois
FRED W. ROEWEKAMP,	Los Angeles, California

Alpine Firs

* * * * and memories, that dusk distills,
Like lengthening shadows on an highland lake
Cupped in a hollow of the silent hills. — JOHN PHELPS

Photograph by Lloyd R. Koenig,
Courtesy
"American Forests Magazine."

Let's Go to the Park!

"LET'S go to the Park!" Little children say it. Young athletes say it. Tired fathers and mothers say it when the day's work is done. Old men and women dream of it. No one is too young, no one is too old to glow at the thought.

What makes of a Park a place of delight to the young and of refreshment to all? The shade of trees, the coolness of wind over water, the fragrance of flowers, the restfulness of long vistas and winding paths, the music of running water, the color of sky and grass and tree and flower, and people everywhere at their best, the irritations and disappointments of the day no longer uppermost in their minds, a place to play or to rest and relax in the beauty of the outdoors—we all enjoy these things. We all are the better for them.

But do we think how they have come to be, whose thought and work and care have provided them for us, and what we ourselves can do to preserve them and to increase the service they render to all who will come?

Purpose of Parks

WHEN asked why we have Parks, most people reply, "for safe and convenient places for young folks to exercise and to play." Undoubtedly this is one of the most important reasons.

If everyone lived in the country where there were miles between houses, the only time they would need a park would be for their Fourth of July picnic and celebration. Those appointed on the committee to choose a desirable picnic spot would search for a beautiful wooded area with a stream flowing through it or with a lake near by. The only improvements they would make on such a place would be the building of a road to make it accessible and the cutting down of weeds. Certainly they would not think of doing more than was absolutely necessary to make the grounds usable for their celebration. Probably during the rest of the year the grounds would serve as Farmer Jones' pasture, and children would play in the fields and orchards surrounding their own homes.

But everybody does not live in the country. Many live in towns and cities. The children who live in towns and cities need to play just as much as do the young folks of the country. They need it more. Work on a farm is largely activity in the out-of-doors. Children, even the smallest, find opportunity for physical exercise in the natural course of the day's chores — chicken-raising, gardening, driving the cows — all those activities that to city children spell *play* of entrancing charm.

Congested city areas and the types of work that create them do not provide an outlet for nervous energy or relief from the strain of city life. Town lots and city apartments give no stretch for even a decent run, no neccessary and happy outdoor activities for as much as an hour a day.

The pent-up energies of childhood and youth must have an outlet. If this cannot be in clean, wholesome sports and outdoor activities, it will be in less desirable ways. It is in congested areas with no adequate play spaces that crime most flourishes and criminals are made. Most criminals are young fellows of an age to which sports make the greatest appeal. Police records show a marked decrease in crime and juvenile delinquency where an adequate park has been opened up in a congested area. It is estimated that crime costs every American citizen $1.50 per month. One hundred twenty-five million people and $1.50 per month means $187,500,000 a month —a sum that would build, equip and maintain many parks.

If the slum areas of our towns and big cities cause so much crime,

Ernest L. Crandall
Courtesy "American Forests"

The Glory of Birches — There They Stand To Grace The Hillside

The artistry of winter has hung with heavy ermine these great trees in the Yosemite. And the camera—in a split second—transcribes a view winter has worked for months to produce.

The wild ducks seek Boise's Sanctuary (Idaho).

During the last few years, the Government has established bird sanctuaries in all parts of the country. In this way our wild life is protected from the hunters.

Courtesy "Parks and Recreation."

and crime is so expensive for everyone, why is not something done about it? Why are these areas not torn down and rebuilt? That is exactly what our Government is beginning to do. Block after block of old buildings is being wrecked, and in their places beautiful new buildings are being constructed with enough ground around them or near them for play areas. This is a far better way to invest public money than to continue to spend huge sums to keep criminals in jail or to maintain large police forces to prevent crime. It makes the children and the adults who live in these sections happier, and better citizens as well.

This idea of making better citizens probably has been the chief motive of those people who are interested in establishing parks as city playgrounds. The sense of joint ownership in a place of beauty not only deters children from committing acts of vandalism, but leads them to resent such acts on the part of others—thus developing in them a respect for property, which is most needful and which it is impossible to develop in one who has nothing to call his own.

People who promoted the idea of building city parks say that surrounding people's homes with beauty leads them to love beauty so much that they no longer will permit ugliness to exist around them. Loving beauty, they themselves become better people—their lives become more beautiful too.

Photograph by R. C. M. for Fort Worth Park Department.

BOYS IN THE ALLEY

A familiar scene down the alley in any large city is a group of boys "shooting craps". Dice and alleys so frequently go together and often result in making criminals of boys and girls who are forced to live in such an environment.

Too often when building our cities we failed to provide playgrounds for our citizens. We thought every foot of ground must be used commercially—that we could not afford to give land for play and recreation. But contrast this scene with what is happening today, as shown in the picture on the opposite page.

There is also the idea of equalizing opportunities for physical and mental health. For the most part, man is a creature of the outdoors. It is not natural for him to live in surroundings of stone, cement and brick. In the noise and confusion of the modern city, his delicate nervous system is under a terrific strain. Were it not for the fact that he can retreat to the park or the country, his physical condition would be vitally impaired. It is common to hear people who have visited parks say that to walk along a nature trail is to receive a tonic more effective than any other they have experienced.

Parks, then, are valuable from the standpoint of recreation, of good citizenship, of maintenance of physical and mental health. They serve as one means of making life more beautiful. They have a further use.

A great problem of today is the protection of wild life. Already many native species are nearly extinct. Every child knows that but for the fact that no shooting is allowed in parks, the squirrels and

BOYS AND SWANS

Instead of alleys and narrow streets in which to play, many of our citizens are being given playgrounds and beautiful parks.

Along with the creation of more abundant beauty there should develop a greater appreciation of trees, flowers and animals; and with this development there should come a richer culture, that will lead to a happier life for all our people.

Photograph by R. C. M. for Fort Worth Park Department.

birds would soon be gone. Where parks are properly developed and protected, wild life has an opportunity to multiply and to live unharmed.

People who are interested in parks believe also what natural beauty the country has should be preserved, so that a hundred years from now it may still be a joy to all who see. Preceding generations have left these beauties for us to enjoy. We would be very selfish if we thought only of ourselves and destroyed our forests and neglected our lakes and streams. Yet that is exactly what has happened in too many sections of this country. Where natural beauty of gorge or waterfall, rocks or woodlands is endangered, citizens now find it necessary to buy the surrounding land to preserve its natural beauty as a permanent possession.

Parks are not luxuries or merely something nice to have. They are necessary parts of every town and city, and a vital part of every family's experience.

The History of Public Parks

THE public park seems to have originated in the union of three ideas from three different countries of ancient civilization.

The idea of parks began to assume definiteness in Egypt, where even the poor man had his tiny garden and bit of shady grove, where each temple was surrounded by its sacred trees, and where each court official built a private park on his own estate. In the Metropolitan Museum of Art in New York City is a model of an Egyptian temple garden dating from 2000 B. C. In a restored tomb at Thebes is pictured the plan of a nobleman's park dating from 1500 B. C. Pools were freely used in these parks, one being a mile long and nearly 1,000 feet wide—large enough for boating.

The Egyptian parks were private, as were those in Babylonia and Assyria where they were used chiefly as hunting-preserves. Trees were so highly prized there that the worst punishment which could be visited upon an enemy was to cut down his tree.

The most famous gardens in Babylonia were the Hanging Gardens built by a Babylonian king to please his wife who wept for the green hills of her native land. These gardens covered three acres and were built like a stadium, with stepped-back terraces supported by arches whose pillars were four feet thick. Steps led from one terrace to the next. Under the terraces were the royal chambers, each facing a sixteen foot garden terrace.

The first semblance of a public use of parks appeared in ancient Persia where the nobles sometimes permitted the common people to enjoy some of the benefits of their hunting-parks.

Centuries later, in India, the Buddhist priests opened their sacred groves as public places for rest and contemplation. According to Richardson Wright, in his "Story of Gardening," these groves were to be "not too near the town, not too far away, well provided with entrances, easily reached by the people who are like to come, not too noisy by day, perfectly quiet by night, removed from disturbances and crowds, a place of retreat and lonely contemplation."

The third of the three ideas which together seem to form the beginning of the public park idea came from Greece.

KITES AND A PLACE
TO FLY THEM

If every community were planned properly there would be open spaces left for such good, wholesome recreation as flying kites. Not only would our cities be more beautiful and our property values stabilized, but we would produce citizens of higher order and we would have fewer policing bills.

Photogaph by R. C. M. for Fort Worth Park Department.

The Persian park was the rich man's domain, which he frequently permitted the public to use. The Buddhist grove was the property of the priests who opened it to public contemplation and recreation. The Greek public park was the possession of the people from the beginning. Here the first public games were played. In time it became a spot of great beauty with plane-tree alleys bordered with shrubs and narrow paths called philosophers' walks. It was enriched with marble-edged water canals, and in one part was a long

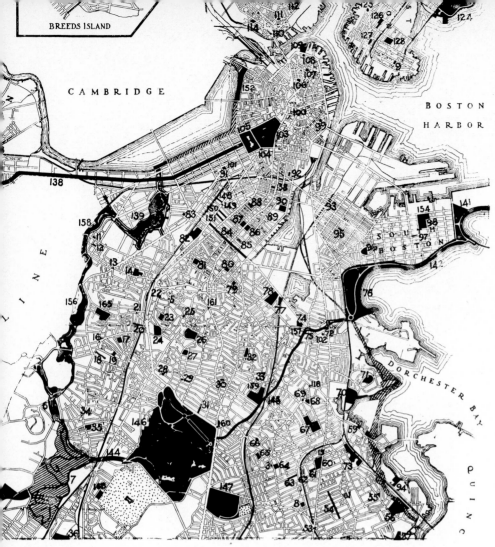

BREEDS ISLAND

CAMBRIDGE

BOSTON HARBOR

SOUTH BOSTON

DORCHESTER BAY

POINT

BOSTON PARK AND FENWAY PLAN

The black areas indicate park sites. Notice how they are distributed over the entire city and how the larger parks are connected by a park drive.

Courtesy "Parks and Recreation."

oval race-course. In these public parks or groves, outdoor schools began. For a time Aristotle taught in one, as did Plato and Epicurus. Here was finally evolved the idea of an area that belonged to everyone, where people could come together for whatever purpose they desired.

In Rome, the poor had the run of the public parks, many of which were created by the various emperors. Augustus provided a park containing a public recreation area around the tomb which he built for himself. The mausoleum of Hadrian was ringed about with terraced gardens. Caesar willed to the public his parks and gardens, including a game area and much statuary. At the end of the third century A. D., Rome had eight commons for public games and thirty public parks. In addition, the commoners could enjoy the gardens of the temple-groves, the cemeteries and the baths.

Except in connection with the monasteries, neither public nor private parks could flourish in Europe during the Dark Ages when life was hedged in to the restricted grounds of a walled castle or a fortified town. But in India during this time both private and public parks were developed. One monarch alone, Feroz Shali (1321-88), is said to have created one hundred parks around Delhi, each equipped with bathing-tanks and baths.

Parks flourished also in China where Kublai Khan in 1325 had deer and other animal preserves, the first Chinese arboretum stocked with plants and trees from the length and breadth of his domain, and a park containing a huge artificial lake. He established many great public gardens in various parts of his realm.

The rise of rich cities in Europe and the comparative security of

FRANKLIN PARK, BOSTON.

One of the characteristics of the works of Frederick Law Olmsted was the creation of the meadow surrounded by heavy foliage.

THE CHARLES RIVER
BASIN
(Boston)

A close view of the lagoon. All land along rivers and lakes should be owned or controlled by the city.

the Renaissance renewed interest in both private and public parks, especially in the type of park known as Botanic Gardens. The first of these was founded in Spain in 1555. The idea spread rapidly until in 1685 the Dutch East India Company had opened one in its colony at the Cape of Good Hope.

Everywhere the nobility of every land created parks as settings for pompous living. The great Gardens of Versailles, designed for Louis XIV by Le Notre in 1662 are an outstanding example.

Probably of more direct influence on American parks was the idea of the Commons as developed in English village life. Each villager had a little farm outside the village which he cultivated, but there was also land that was left for common pasturage for all the cattle of the village. This land was called the village commons. There the children played, and there the young people disported themselves at the close of the day. Even in the Middle Ages, the commoners (those who used the commons) had set up certain rules or regulations so that the land could not be destroyed by a few selfish people. No one had a right to lop trees and ruin their beauty. The dominant thought was to use the land wisely and as sparingly as possible, so that its value might be preserved.

Our forefathers, being of English descent, brought with them to this country the idea that every town should have a commons. Nearly all of the colonial towns and cities of New England had a commons. The best known, of course, is Boston Commons.

As one reads history, he is impressed by the fact that man is essentially a lover of nature, and that he always has wanted his cities to be Garden Cities. In 1682, William Penn wrote, in directing the commissioners who settled his colony in Pennsylvania, to see that every house "be placed, if the Person please, in ye middle of its place as to the breadth way of it, so that there may be grounds on each side, for gardens, or orchards, or fields, yet it may be a greene Country Towne, which will never be burnt and will always be wholesome." Five public squares were laid out within the town's limits, and in the center was a square of ten acres. These squares corresponded to the commons of New England villages.

The same sort of scheme was followed in Georgia and South Carolina in the following century, so that everywhere in this country the idea of common land and open squares was prevalent. When L'Enfant drew the plan for the Capital City of the United States in George Washington's time, it surprised no one that it called for beautiful parks and for lovely settings for the public buildings.

Other cities, as their areas extended, sought to expand their parks into larger units. In 1853, the City of New York prepared for an expansion which should cover Manhattan Island and which should contain a central park of noble proportions. A competition for the design of this park was conducted. It was won by Frederick Law Olmsted and his partner, Mr. Vaux.

THE CHARLES RIVER BASIN (Boston)

Courtesy "Parks and Recreation."

THE MUSIC OVAL
When this is in operation, it is filled with portable chairs—thousands of them —furnished by the Commission for a very small charge. Permanent seats are not needed. The two arcs of a circle in The Basin are the breakwater, twenty feet wide, surfaced with very coarse gravel and heavy stonework and laid on a 2—1 slope, but there is no masonry and no cement. Willow-trees are planted by driving stakes into the stonework. The distant bridge is the beautiful Longfellow Bridge, built about 1903 and carried high in air to avoid the use of a drawbridge as required by the U. S. Government Engineers.

13]

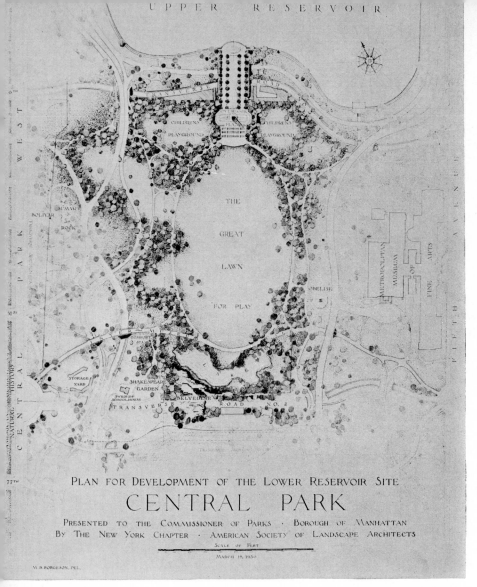

PLAN FOR DEVELOPMENT OF THE LOWER RESERVOIR SITE
CENTRAL PARK
PRESENTED TO THE COMMISSIONER OF PARKS · BOROUGH OF MANHATTAN
BY THE NEW YORK CHAPTER · AMERICAN SOCIETY OF LANDSCAPE ARCHITECTS
SCALE OF FEET
MARCH 15, 1930

Courtesy "Parks and Recreation."

Today the wisdom of our forefathers in setting aside an open space within a congested metropolitan area is ever evident.

Central Park, New York City, will forever stand as a monument to its great designers, Frederick Law Olmsted and his partner, Mr. Vaux.

This plan for the development of the lower reservoir site in Central Park was made by the New York Chapter of the American Society of Landscape Architects.

Mr. Olmsted is often spoken of as America's first landscape architect, and 1853 is often referred to as the date when the profession of landscape architecture in this country began. Through the winning of this competition and the laying out of Central Park, with its lakes and steep rocks, its great meadows and its heavy border-plantings which shut out the busy city, Mr. Olmsted became very famous. Other cities wanted him to lay out their parks. Between 1853 and 1900 he laid out Riverside Park, New York, —a long, narrow park along the Hudson River from 72nd Street to Grant's Tomb; Morningside Park, which features the rocky steep known in

Revolutionary Days as Harlem Heights; Prospect Park in Brooklyn, with its long approach and its fine view of the Narrows and of New York Harbor; Delaware Park in Buffalo, with its man-made lake in rolling country; Fairmount Park in Philadelphia, with its thousand acres of ravine; the grounds surrounding the Capitol at Washington; and he made out of a bare stretch of lake front the fairylike park which was the setting for the Chicago Fair of 1893.

There have been other great builders of parks in this country. One, a contemporary of Mr. Olmsted in his later years, was Mr. Charles Eliot whose father was the famous president of Harvard University. Mr. Eliot is largely responsible for the wonderful Park System of Boston, Massachusetts, with its drives connecting the individual parks, its boulevard-plantings and its Fenway through the heart of the city which preserves the natural beauty of the famous Frog Pond, in direct contrast to the tendency of most cities to fill in or cover up low-lying lands like these.

Somewhat later, in the Middle West, another landscape architect became known. He was George Kessler of Kansas City, Missouri, who did much to promote the park idea in many midwestern cities. Today one may see his many works in the great cities of this area.

In Chicago, one of the early landscape architects was Jens Jensen who helped create Chicago's marvelous Park System. Built on flat, swampy ground, Chicago has made her parks more interesting by creating artificial knolls and making wide use of lagoons and pools. The separate parks are connected by parkways from 300 to

LARGE SWIMMING-
POOLS AT
COLUMBUS PARK,
CHICAGO

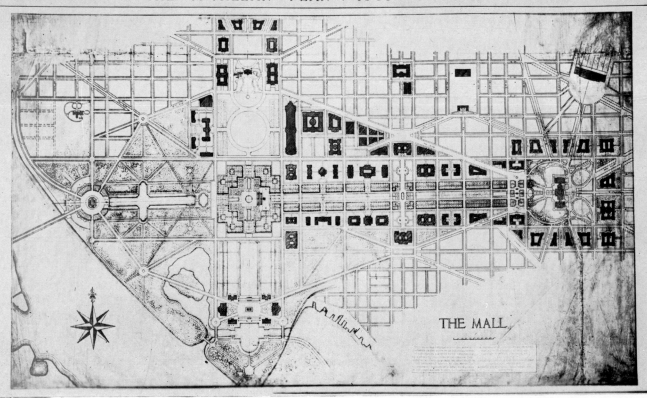

THE MALL

Although the City of Washington was planned from the beginning, our citizens did little to carry out the suggestions of its designers.

1000 feet wide along the boulevards, providing ample open areas for general recreation. Miles and miles of parkways and parks now help make living more pleasant in that large city. Were it not for parks in such large cities, few people would care to live in them. They are the redeeming features where congestion is so common.

To these men America owes her gratitude for having started the idea of the great American park. Their lifework has been the creation of parks. As cities grow and people have more leisure time, parks will become more and more important.

Model of our Capital City showing the Mall, bordered by planting and monumental public buildings.

Our people allowed such conditions as are pictured above to exist instead of following the original plan to make Washington a beautiful city throughout.

Finally, during late years, we have torn down many shacks and have gone far toward making Washington, D. C., the most beautiful city in the world.

THE MALL

Showing the Arlington Memorial Bridge in the right foreground, the Lincoln Memorial in the center, the Washington Monument and the Capitol in the distance.

(Photograph by U. S. Army Air Corps.)

Were we to choose a park site we would certainly want all the land around a lake. This picture shows the Lake of the Isles, Minneapolis, Minnesota.

Selection of Park Sites

In almost every town and city there are certain natural features which make that city different from any other. If these areas are owned by the city and are preserved, they not only will give pleasure to all the people but will make a unique contribution to the reputation of the city.

Perhaps it is a river that runs through the town. If its banks are privately owned, they may be covered with billboards and ugly shacks with neglected areas between them. If the community owns them, a park can be developed with drives on each side of the river so that everyone may enjoy the beauty that the river affords.

In Europe, nearly all cities have followed this plan. There are beautifully shaded drives on either side of the river, with shops and stores facing the parkway which is the beauty spot of the town. Cambridge and Boston have developed the banks of the Charles River in a similar way, with trees and flowers and seats in the shade. The river is gay with boating and water-sports, and here the boat crew of Harvard University does its work. In New York State, there existed for many years a very ugly spot along a little stream known as Bronx River. It was privately owned and was filled with old buildings, billboards and dumping-grounds. Hundreds of thousands of people saw it every day as they rode to and from their work

THE ALAMO, SAN ANTONIO, TEXAS

In the heart of San Antonio stands The Alamo. The grounds around the historic building are set aside as a park. Every city should preserve its historic sites as public parks as well as shrines for our citizens to visit.

Beginnings of the South Park Commissioners' Made-Land Park Development looking toward the World's Fair, Chicago, 1933.

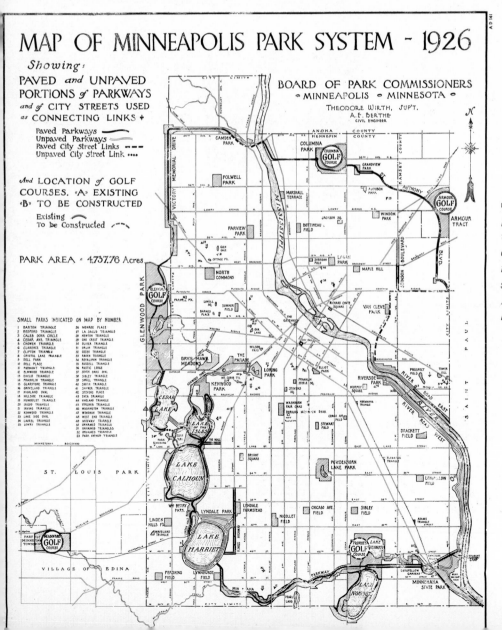

Many of our progressive cities have developed a comprehensive Park System, where the larger park areas are connected by a beautiful park drive. The map shows the Minneapolis Park System which has become world famous.

in New York City. At last the people of New York bought this land and made of it a long parkway which has come to be one of the most beautiful in all the world.

Or there may be a lake. Chicago is beautifully situated upon Lake Michigan. But, in the days before she awoke to the need for beauty and open spaces, she permitted industries and railroads to usurp the lake-front. She has spent millions of dollars to raise the lake-front above the tracks, cover them over, and build land beyond, from the lake itself, for her most beautiful park and fountain. Madison and Minneapolis are two cities encircling a number of little lakes. Every city so blessed should own all the shoreline and maintain it as a park.

In other cities there are high bluffs or hills that afford wonderful views of the surrounding country. San Francisco has such hills in the center of the city, beautifully wooded, with drives running through. Kansas City has cliffs and high bluffs overlooking a valley, —land undesirable from the standpoint of the builder and the real

Courtesy Minneapolis Park Department.

TO WHOM DOES THE RIVER BELONG?

By Howard Braucher

To whom does the river belong?
 To the boy and girl in the canoe, gliding along
  in the moonlight.
To whom is the bay and its islands and the rocky
   shore line?
 To him who silently sails it.
Who has leased the ocean?
 He who swims it, jumps its breakers, who knows
  it at midnight and midday, who understands
  its many voices.
Who has most shares in the sun?
 He who takes time to bathe his body in its
  rays.
In whose name is the deed to the woods?
 In his name who tramps it, who wades its
  brooks, who sees its wild flowers and reads
  its signs.

Who owns the mountain?
 He who climbs it and lies on its summit and
  watches the clouds go by.
To whom does the craft of the world belong?
 To him who knows and can use the tools, who
  can see and understand its beauty.
For whom are the gardens?
 For those whose hands love the soil, whose eyes
  can watch the growth from day to day, for
  those who lose themselves in its beauty.
For whom are the books and the thoughts of all
  ages?
 For those who can read and for those who can
  think.
For whom is the music, for whom is the art of
  the world?
 For those who can hear it, for those who can
  see it.

Salem, Massachusetts, has been wise to make a public park of such a fine water-front as we
see pictured above. Thousands use this park each year for boating and bathing.

Cape Cod is one of the most popular summer resorts in America. There the value of preserving the water-front for recreation purposes is indeed apparent to all.
This map was drawn and published by B. Ashburton Tripp, Landscape Architect.

A typical picnic-ground in Los Angeles, California.

Here the city has acquired much of the low land for park purposes, as it is on such sites that we find the finest trees.

estate broker, but easily landscaped into the ten-mile drive, winding around cliffs and over high bluffs, which is the pride of that city.

Or the city may have low, swampy land with stagnant watercourses subject to overflow, which under usual conditions would be used for dumps and flimsy structures. Of little value for business or residence purposes, this land is the very best from the standpoint of the landscape architect. In the South there is much land of this type, and it is here that most of the beautiful native trees are found. The only way to preserve them and to make an asset of this area is to turn it into a park site, using drains and dams to produce a lake and free-flowing stream. In this way, a double service is rendered the city—the elimination of a municipal nuisance, frequently of a dangerous character, and the creation of a place of beauty. Where such areas have been developed as parks, the value of the surrounding property has risen to such an extent that the increase in taxes has been sufficient to pay for the park improvements.

In some counties there are large stands of trees which help to break the winds and to regulate the temperature and rainfall of the area around them, and which can be preserved and at the same time

On Point Fermin Park, overlooking the Pacific Ocean, Los Angeles, California, has built this interesting picnic pergola.

Courtesy Paul Riis.

A CAMPER'S PRAYER

God of the hills, grant me Thy strength to go back
  to the cities without faltering,
Strength to do my daily task without tiring, and
  with enthusiasm;
Strength to help my neighbor, who has no hills to
  remember.
God of the lake, grant me Thy peace and Thy restfulness;
Peace, to bring into the world of hurry and confusion;
Restfulness, to carry to the tired ones whom I shall
  meet every day.
Content to do small things with a freedom from
  littleness,
Self-control for the unexpected emergency and pa-
  tience for the wearisome task,
With deep depths within my soul to bear with me
  through crowded places.
The hush of the night-time, when the pine-trees
  are dark against the sky-line,
The humbleness of the hills, which, in their mighti-
  ness, know it not,
And the laughter of the sunny days to brighten the
  cheerless spots in winter.
God of the stars, may I take back the gift of friend-
  ship and love for all;
Fill me with great tenderness for the needy person
  at every turning;
May I live out the truths which Thou hast taught
  me, through every thought and word and deed.

—MARIAN GRIEVES.

be used as recreation-areas. Cook County, in which Chicago is located, owns large stretches of such forest preserves. Less fortunate areas, whose groves have been cut down, and those without native woodlands, suffer much from wind-storms, and recently, as in Kansas, from dust-storms which strip the top soil and ruin the farm-areas. To combat this condition in the West, the Federal Government has sponsored the planting of thousands of trees.

All of these areas which have just been mentioned as desirable and economical for park sites affect the town and city dweller principally. There are other types of land that should be made into parks controlled by the National Government for the benefit of all the people of the whole country. These are the scenic spots of the country, such as the snow-capped mountains in Rocky Mountain National Park, the big trees of the Sequoia Forests, the great waterfall and many-colored canyon of the Yellowstone, and the Carlsbad Caverns in New Mexico. The Federal Government is fast taking over such natural wonders as these.

Looking across Swope Park, Kansas City, Missouri, from the Mauseoleum.

Today there are 22 National Parks — a total area of 12,000 square miles — which are administered by the National Park Service, and 59 related reservations known as National Monuments, of which 32 are administered by the National Park Service.

A National Park, according to the Act of Congress in 1916 which established the National Park Service, is an area of unusual scenic beauty or natural phenomena set aside by Congress "to conserve its scenery and the natural and historic objects and the wild life therein, and to provide for the enjoyment of the same in such a manner and by such means as will leave them unimpaired for the enjoyment of future generations."

National Monuments are reservations established by Presidential proclamation under the authority granted him by Congress in 1906 "to declare by public proclamation historic landmarks, historic or prehistoric structures, and objects of historic or scientific interest that are situated upon land owned or controlled by the Government of the United States to be National Monuments."

The chart at the end of this book will show the location of these National Parks and Monuments, together with the area of each.

The Cliff Drive in Kansas City, Missouri, is one of the city's finest assets.

The general administrative work for the National Parks is carried on in an office in Washington, but there are three field divisions — educational, civil engineering and landscape architecture — with headquarters in San Francisco.

Each Park is in charge of its own Superintendent and is protected and cared for by a corps of rangers. Most of them are equipped with hotel and lodge accommodations for travelers and with free public camping-grounds which have water and electric lights. Firewood is provided and, in some places, open fireplaces for cooking. There are roads and trails through the parks, saddle-horses and autos, and, where possible, ski courses, sleighs and snowshoes.

The great increase in the number of visitors to these parks — a tenfold increase between 1916 and 1928 — has led to the tentative

Every city should own much of the natural beauty for park purposes. In this way, the trees would never be cut down for private use, but would stand for the enjoyment of everyone. This is what Minneapolis, Minnesota, has done. They call the pine-tree in this picture "The Lonesome Pine," which grows in Minnehaha Parkway.

Courtesy Minneapolis Park Department.

development of a National Park-to-Park Highway 4,500 miles long, which brings into connection all the National Parks of the West. It is not yet wholly paved. Many hope that a road of this nature may be extended to the National Parks in other parts of the country and that the whole may be developed into a scenic tourway equipped with rest-houses and adjacent camping-sites.

Recently the Federal Government has developed a new policy in what they call their Program of Rural Rehabilitation, in which all the land not well adapted to agriculture will be developed by the Civilian Conservation Corps as National Park areas. There is much land in this country not suitable for the production of crops, but entirely suitable for reforestation and recreation purposes.

A further step in the development of parks and recreation-areas

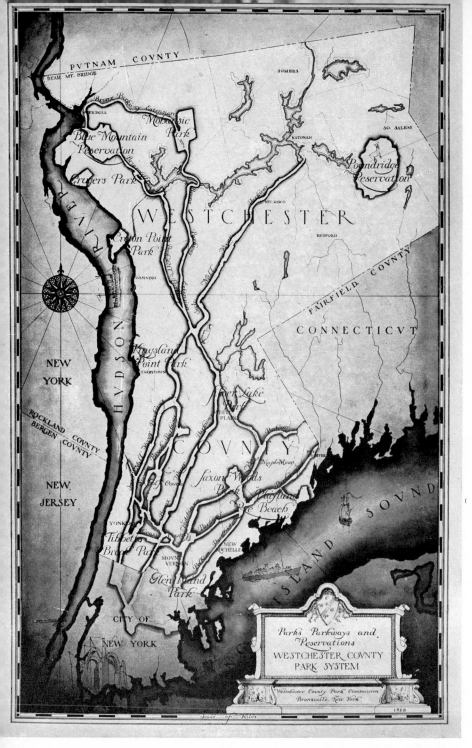

Map of Westchester County showing lands acquired for Parks, Parkways and Reservations by the Westchester County Park Commission.

One can now drive from New York City to Bear Mountain over one of the most beautiful parkways in the world.

Courtesy "Parks and Recreation."

on a national scale was taken by Congress in the Act approved June 23, 1936, which provides that the Secretary of the Interior be directed to cause the National Park Service to "make a comprehensive study of the public park, parkway and recreation-area programs

Hutchinson River Parkway, Westchester County, New York. (Paved 40 feet wide—graded so that 20 additional feet of pavement may be added.)

Originally, much of this land was used as a dumping-ground. Today, the value of land along this development is m u c h higher than it was before the improvement.

Photograph by John Gass.

Gilmore D. Clarke, Landscape Architect.

Courtesy Westchester County Park Commission.

of the United States, and of the several States and political subdivisions thereof, and of the lands throughout the United States which are or may be chiefly valuable as such areas * * * for the purpose of developing coördinated and adequate public park, parkway and recreation-area facilities for the people of the United States."

If the Federal Government and every state and every town and city think hard enough about parks and do enough about them, parks can be within the reach of everyone. But governments can move in this direction, as in every other, only as fast as its citizens permit.

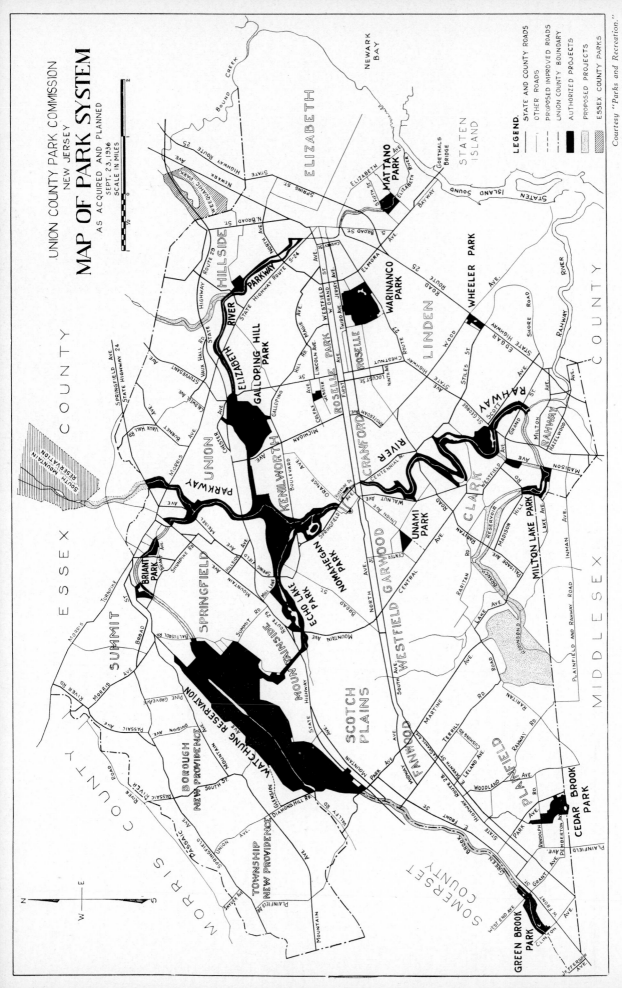

UNION COUNTY PARK COMMISSION
NEW JERSEY

MAP OF PARK SYSTEM

AS ACQUIRED AND PLANNED
SEPT. 23, 1936
SCALE IN MILES

LEGEND

STATE AND COUNTY ROADS
OTHER ROADS
PROPOSED IMPROVED ROADS
UNION COUNTY BOUNDARY
AUTHORIZED PROJECTS
PROPOSED PROJECTS
ESSEX COUNTY PARKS

Courtesy "Parks and Recreation."

Parks and Playgrounds, in great variety, distributed and developed for the use of residential suburban population, based on Greater New York.

As cities grow, it becomes more important that we create a County or Metropolitan Park Department.

[38

The Government is making parks of many such areas as this picture portrays. The farmers are moved to more fertile, and consequently more suitable, land, as part of the work being done through state and regional land-planning.

Devastation marks the depths of a cycle of unwise use of land. Wind erosion, encouraged by over-grazing and the cultivation of excessively dry lands, has ruined this farm. Typical of many sections in the West.

Below we see the C.C.C. boys protecting the land from erosion by placing rock in the ground to carry away the water, and by planting trees on the slopes. They are also grading a hiking-trail, as you can see by the stakes in the picture.

Courtesy "American Forests."

tesy "American Forests."

Boat on St. Mary Lake — Glacier National Park. Our Federal Government is preserving for all time to come the beauty of many of our mountains.

Marion Creek Fall, Willamette National Forest, Oregon. By the creation of a National Forest, the trees and the waterfalls are protected from commercialization.

Courtesy *"Texas Outlook."*

The C.C.C. boys have built a very beautiful shelter at Mosque Point, Lake Worth, which is the water-supply for Fort Worth, Texas. Miles of hiking-trails have also been made for the recreation of the people.

Organization of a City Park Department

When one drives through beautiful parks and enjoys the wonderful trees, flowers and shrubs, when he visits the zoo, when he watches the games that are being played, he seldom realizes that behind all these things there must be some sort of organization, some group of people that has been empowered to provide these things for us. Everything we have in our cities that is worthwhile and lovely is the result of long years of planning on the part of some one person or some group of persons. Fine things do not just happen. They are made to happen by people who care, people who want everybody to enjoy living and to be happy.

This is certainly true of parks. Usually a Park Department is created at a public meeting called by a group of interested citizens to which other interested citizens come. At this meeting, arrangements are made which lead to the election or appointment of a Park Board.

Members of this Board serve without pay, and, being merchants or doctors or engineers with businesses of their own to look after, they can give but a few hours each week to Park business. Not one of them has been trained to know how to get the best Park System for the least money. Therefore one of the first things the Board does is to hire a trained man as Park Superintendent.

The Park Superintendent makes a survey of the layout of the city, looking for available park sites. If the community is small, he may be the only specially trained man in the Park Department. The other employees will be able to do only what he tells them to do.

Planting the city streets with trees evenly spaced and of like varieties is one of the duties of the Forestry Department.

The picture shows a street in Galveston, Texas, planted with palm-trees.

Courtesy *"Southern Home and Garden."* Photo by R. C. M.

Some work of the Park Department will go undone, since it is impossible for one man to be thoroughly expert in landscape architecture, engineering, forestry, horticulture, public recreation and all the other professions that enter into the building and maintenance of parks.

Large cities employ, besides the Park Superintendent, a Landscape Architect. He is an artist who designs parks, working with trees and shrubs as other artists work with paint-brush or chisel. He knows plants and the effects that can be produced with them as they change from season to season. He knows nature's processes and materials and how to work with them. He plans the layout of the park, plots its walks and drives, its playfields and gardens, and determines the plantings that make of it a thing of beauty. Since he

Courtesy "Parks and Recreation."

Irregular Street Tree Planting on a Curved Avenue—Lake of the Isles Boulevard, Minneapolis. Every city should have a Forestry Department to plant and care for the trees on all main boulevards and parkways.

cannot carry out his designs with his own hand, he must be able to convey his ideas—not by means of words only, but by drawings, reports and specifications—to those who are to execute the work. Smaller places employ such a man for only part time, as new park areas are under consideration.

The Landscape Engineer carries out the plans of the Landscape

Courtesy Chicago Park Department.

The "fern house" at Garfield Park Conservatory, Chicago, provides a tropical garden that is enjoyed by thousands of people each year.

Courtesy Los Angeles Park Department.

The city of Los Angeles has planted palms on the Vermont Avenue parkway.

Architect to the smallest detail of curve and grading, and of planting.

It avails little to build beautiful parks if care is not given to their maintenance and protection. Two specially trained men share this work,—the City Forester and the Horticulturist.

The City Forester watches over the trees of the parks and of the city streets as well.

Every street should be lined with trees. Trees give shade, they relieve the monotony of pavement and masonry. They purify the

Courtesy Chicago Park Department.

Every year the Park Department of Chicago has a magnificent chrysanthemum show in its Garfield Park Conservatory.

Street trees play an important part in the civic picture. East meets West in the use of the Oriental Plane tree in Sacramento, California. Note how unity of effect is attained by use of one variety on street.

air and protect from wind. They do more than any other one thing to beautify a city. If properly planted and cared for, they are its greatest asset.

Trees are especially subject to injury and destruction by disease and insect pests. From 1918 to 1924, nearly all the chestnut-trees in the East were killed by chestnut-blight. Then came the gypsy-moth and, in recent years, the Japanese elm-beetle to cause much trouble, and now elm-blight threatens to destroy all of the beautiful old elms. In the South, bag-worms and stinging-asps and root-rot damage trees to the extent of hundreds of thousands of dollars. The live-oak, most beloved tree in the South, in 1933 was afflicted with a new disease, oak-tree blight.

No one would guess this lovely garden is in the far northern part of our country where, outside, there are ice and snow much of the year.

It is the garden in the Como Park Conservatory, St. Paul, Minnesota.

The Park Department of every city should provide its citizens with outdoor theaters.

This picture shows the outdoor theater in Pasadena, California.

Outside the Municipal Conservatory in Como Park, St. Paul, Minnesota.

Every city should have a beautifully designed Rose Garden. This Garden is in Elizabeth Park, Hartford, Connecticut. Hartford was one of the first cities in America to have such a Garden, and every year thousands of people go there to see the many varieties of roses.

Courtesy "Parks and Recreation."

All these diseases and insect pests must be controlled by the City's Forestry Department, since it is obvious that it would be useless for an individual citizen to attempt to protect his own trees if infected trees all around him are left uncared for.

Trees in our cities are further endangered by the smoke from industries and the gas from automobiles. They need the scientific care of a City Forester.

The City Forester not only protects trees in parks and on city property; he gives advice throughout the city on the planting and pruning of trees. Trees should be planted far enough apart so that the sun can reach the lawns. They should be in line with one another so that the streets may be orderly. If trees are not pruned sufficiently high, the branches obstruct traffic. If dead wood is allowed to remain in them, they become dangerous to passers-by.

"He is happiest who hath power
To gather wisdom from a flower."

A B

C D

Courtesy *"Texas Outlook."*

Today Garden Clubs are establishing Garden Centers where there is kept literature on all subjects pertaining to gardening. This is a picture of the Garden Center in Fort Worth, Texas, which is sponsored by the Board of Education together with the Garden Club and the Fort Worth Board of Park Commissioners. The building is located in the Fort Worth Botanic Garden. Here classes from the public schools are given instruction in horticulture, and much is done to make them "park-minded."

Los Angeles, California, has a beautiful Conservatory that displays plants from all parts of the world.

Courtesy Los Angeles Park Department.

The Horticulturist cares for the Botanic Gardens and flower-beds and greenhouses of the parks. He also gives free advice to citizens on the creation and care of their own flower-beds and gardens. In smaller places, the City Forester or the Park Superintendent does this work.

One of the most popular features of a park is a Zoo. This requires the services of a man who knows animals and their ways, how to feed them and keep them clean and comfortable in captivity, and how to care for them if they are ill.

One of the main purposes of parks being to provide the opportunity for recreation for all, the need for a Recreation Director is clear. He plans the details of the operation of playgrounds, ballfields and swimming-pools, providing instruction where needed.

Courtesy Los Angeles Park Department.

Nearly all of t *principal streets* *Los Angeles are we* *planted by the Pa* *Department.*

This is a view *Occidental B o u l e* *vard.*

Courtesy "Parks and Recreation."

But this is not all. A long time ago people learned that "an idle mind is the devil's workshop", — that a person with nothing to do usually gets into trouble. It has been said that it is not what one does while he works that counts so much as what he does when he is not working. Too often people think that free time is meant for loafing. But the person who loafs does not have nearly as much fun out of life as does the person with a special interest or hobby, and the world is never made better by a loafer.

The Recreation Director encourages everyone to plan something interesting to do — to have a hobby. Some people study flowers as a hobby. Think what an interesting time a person could have collecting all the wild flowers of the state and learning their names, or growing a great variety of iris or waterlilies. Just imagine

Courtesy "Parks and Recreation."

Working on the Lion Grotto at the Chicago Zoological Park.

Cement is poured to look like natural rock.

RECREATION FACILITIES - THE UNION COUNTY PARK SYSTEM - 1936

Playgrounds	Baseball Fields	Softball Fields	Soccer Fields	Football Fields	Field Hockey Areas	Tennis Courts	Golf Course (27 holes)	Cricket Fields	Bowling Greens	Handball Courts	Quoit Courts	Horseshoe Courts	Fireplaces	Lakes	Fishing Areas	Boating Areas	Canoeing Areas	Canoe Storage	Ice-Skating Areas	Hockey Rinks	Swimming Pools	Sand Beaches	Wading Pools	Stadium & Athlet. F'ld	Refectories	Fl'd Houses & Shelters	Camps	Band Stands	Traps (Trapshooting)	Pistol & Rifle Range	Riding Stable	Bridle Paths (Miles)	Nature Trails	Archery Ranges	Gardens	Bocce Courts	Total	PARKS
2	4	9	4	3	1	10					2		6	7	2	2	1		2	1			1	1	1	2	2							2	1	2	69	Warinanco
1	1	4										2	19	2	4	2			2	1			1		2	3	1									1	46	Echo Lake
1	1	1	1	1	1	4		1				2	6	1	1				1	1					1	2	1							1	1	4	33	Cedar Brook
1	1	1	1	1				1				6	3	2	2	2			2						2	2	1								1		29	Green Brook
1	1												47	3	5	1	1	1	1	2	1				1	7	10				1	22	1		1		106	Watchung Res.
1	1												2	2	1				1						1											1	10	Scotch Pl'ns Sect.
1	1	1	1	1								4	1			1	1		1	1	1				1	2											18	Wheeler
1	2	2	1	1	4							3	3						1						1	1									1	1	22	Mattano
																																						Rahway Riv. Pky
2	1	4	1	1		4		1			2	6	14	2	3				2	1	1	1	1		1	2						1					51	Rahway Sect.
												6	2	4		1			2						1							2					18	Clark Sect.
1		1										2	2			2	2	2		2	1																15	Cranford Sect.
	1											4	1	3					1							3			3	1		2					19	Ken'wth Blvd. S.
1	1	1										2							2						1												8	Springf'ld-Union
													1	2					1																		4	Milton Lake
	2	1										4	1	1					2	1					1												13	Nomahegan
1		1				1						2	2	1											4	5											17	Galloping Hill
1	2	1	1									2	2	1											1	1											12	Unami
1	1											2	2																							1	7	Roselle Park
														1	1				1	1					1	1											6	Briant Park
16	17	30	9	9	6	18	1	3	2	2	21	38	112	21	34	4	4	1	21	8	2	2	5	1	17	35	10	3	3	1	1	29	1	3	10	3	503	TOTALS

This chart will give some idea of the number and variety of recreation facilities that are being provided by the Union County Park System, New Jersey.

knowing all the 3600 varieties of roses or the many thousand varieties of cacti. Gliders and kites, whittling and modeling — there is no end to the possibilities. The world has advanced largely through the results of the hobbies of its people. Thomas Edison studied electricity as a hobby, and as a result the world has changed

(Photo, Philadelphia *Evening Bulletin*.) Courtesy *"Parks and Recreation."*

An amphitheater stage in Fairmount Park, Philadelphia, Pennsylvania.

The wings are formed by a h e m l o c k hedge, trimmed to seven feet. A hedge of prostrate yew will screen the footlights.

The reflecting-pool in front of the stage is an interesting feature of this development.

materially. Luther Burbank loved to grow flowers and plants, and made many experiments in cross-pollination which resulted in the development of many new fruits which we enjoy eating today. Think what would happen if everyone had a hobby. Our world could be made much finer in every way.

If a Park System is large, there are two other officials who can add to its efficiency. The Educational Director controls the Community House, the band-concerts and other entertainments, and is the publicity man who keeps the public informed of such interesting events as special displays in conservatories, Botanic Gardens, zoo or museums, and the time and place of concerts and field-meets.

In the Park Department, as in any large enterprise with many divisions, it is advisable to have a Business Manager who sees that bills are paid and budgets adhered to.

All these divisions of park service offer inviting fields of work for young men interested in the outdoors. Anyone who wishes to make himself efficient in any of these fields must first:—

(a). Accumulate a large store of facts and develop the ability to organize them. Here is the reason for specialized schooling. He might accumulate facts for himself, but he could not in one lifetime acquire the skill in selecting and organizing facts in relation to a given problem so as to arrive at the best possible solution. Good schools save years of experience and give students a broader outlook on their work than the untrained ever attain.

The Park Departments in many cities are providing cultural and educational facilities as well as grounds for wholesome active recreation. Below is the Minneapolis Institute of Arts in Doribus Morrison Park, Minneapolis, Minnesota.

It would be a great pleasure to watch a pageant in the Greek Theater in this Los Angeles Park.

(b). Serve an apprenticeship under an expert already in the field.

(c). Remain all his life a student of his own and allied fields.

If he becomes expert in his own field, he may count on earning a living and enjoying his work. Part of his enjoyment will be incidental. He will enjoy the outdoor life, the intercourse with interesting people, and organizing his work and getting things accomplished. But, if he is really fitted for this work, he will enjoy most the chance to express himself in his work as fully and beautifully as any other artist does in his. And he has the added joy of knowing that by his work he brings pleasure and well-being to hosts of others.

The next time you go through a park, think of all the work it has taken to make such a place and how many men have given their best effort to provide you with such opportunities for pleasure and well-being.

A Traffic Study—Soldier Field, Chicago. View of parking-area, south of stadium, during the game. This great stadium is operated by the Park Department.

The Chicago Park Department has made good use of sculpture in its many park areas. The picture is St. Gaudens' "Lincoln," in Lincoln Park, Chicago, Illinois.

Courtesy *"School Executive."* Photo by R. C. M.

In Fort Worth, Texas, all the school-grounds have been developed as model parks and playgrounds, open the year around, not only for the children but for the parents as well.

All the play-areas have been enclosed with a five-foot chain-link fence, around which shrubs and small trees have been planted. In this way there are no barren recreation-fields to mar the beauty of the neighborhood.

This large school-ground landscaping program has been sponsored by the several Federal work-relief programs, the Fort Worth Independent School District and the Fort Worth Park Department. The firm of Hare & Hare, Kansas City, Missouri, have been the consulting landscape architects.

School-Grounds as Parks

The idea that school-grounds may serve as parks is somewhat new. Too often we find school properties used only for educational purposes and closed to the public after teaching-hours. This means a great waste of public funds and the loss of possible enjoyment.

In nearly all cities, there is great need for neighborhood parks and playgrounds located where children will not be forced to walk or ride long distances to reach them. Where communities already are built up, property is so costly that buying land for parks where people really need them seems out of the question. As a result, children must go without modern playgrounds near home unless the School Board and the Park Board coöperate in making the school-grounds into modern parks.

This has been done on a comprehensive scale in Fort Worth, Texas. School-grounds which were ample for the purpose have been landscaped with shrubbery and pleasant walks, playfields of all kinds, quiet nooks for outdoor classrooms and nature study, and an outdoor amphitheater. In other instances, where the grounds were inadequate for school needs, more land has been added, making possible both increased school facilities and a public recreation-center for after school and evenings. The Park Department supervised the development of the grounds and aids in the maintenance of them. The School Board has charge of the grounds during school hours,

Right:—

East Van Zandt Elementary School, Fort Worth, Texas, before development.

Below:—

Now the same school is an asset to the city and an inspiration to the children attending it.

Photo by R. C. M.

W. C. Stripling Junior High School, Fort Worth, Texas.

but the Recreation Department supervises activities on them after school hours and during vacations.

Dr. N. L. Engelhardt of Columbia University has served as Educational Consultant and has done much to coördinate the landscape development with the huge building program.

Where new buildings are under construction, the Landscape Architect and the Building Architect have coöperated in locating the building and in designing the grounds to fit the design of the building. For example, the outdoor gymnasium is placed near the indoor gymnasium. The kindergarten-rooms open directly upon a small play-area designed especially for the use of little folk.

Walks are planned to give easy access to the building and thus eliminate paths across the lawns. A bicycle court with racks does away with the damage resulting from parking wheels in shrubbery-beds. Playgrounds are substantially fenced to guarantee protection to the children using them, and the fences are masked on the exterior with shrubbery-beds.

School-grounds are often bare and ugly spots because there has been no plan for their development. Where there is no well-defined

The William James Junior High School in Fort Worth, Texas, before development.

The same school after development.

plan, there will be no order. Where there is no order, there is no beauty. One of the main purposes of designing school-grounds is to give order to the use of them. With a well-defined plan, carefully conceived, any school-ground can be transformed into a place of beauty, and every community can have at hand a park providing recreation for one and all.

Most important of all is the inspiration that children receive from surroundings of beauty and orderliness. Many children come from homes with little of either, and receive small inspiration for better things except from their schools. Here is the place to instill

Courtesy "Parks and Recreation."

High School at Wichita, Kansas.

School - grounds, properly landscaped and beautified, furnish examples for the improvement of home-grounds.

Making a Model of the Arlington Heights Senior High School, Fort Worth, Texas. This picture shows the celotex to form the finished grading-work of the 35-acre tract.

EVALINE SELLORS. Sculptress.

into every boy and girl love of beauty, respect for property and an understanding that their community is largely what they help to make it.

Academic training constitutes only a small part of what we take with us when we leave school. Somehow our lives are changed by our environment, somehow our attitudes are shaped by our surroundings. It should be our plan, therefore, to provide our children with school-grounds well designed not merely for use but for beauty as well.

This picture shows the amphitheater, the football field, the vista, the asphalt tennis courts, the clock golf course and the large grass playfield—all enclosed by a 5-foot chain-link fence. The celotex here has been covered with plaster of paris. The lawn effects were created by sprinkling colored sawdust over the plaster after the surface had been coated with shellac. Trees were created from picture-wire dipped in wax. They were then sprinkled with finely cut green paper.

A close-up of the Model of Arlington Heights Senior High School, showing the vista from the shelter-house. To the west of this area are the football field, the amphitheater, the clock golf course and the asphalt tennis courts. To the east of the vista there is a large grass playfield.

A view of the entrance to Arlington Heights Senior High School. A sunken garden containing a large reflecting-pool serves as the main feature.

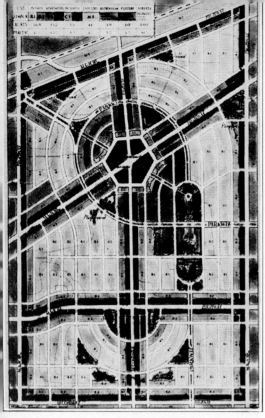

Courtesy *"Southern Home and Garden."*

Those interested in Park development are also interested in City Planning because they know the only way an adequate Park System can be provided is by so designing the city as a whole that large open spaces will be left for recreation areas.

This is a plan for a small community made by the Los Angeles Plan Commission and illustrates the importance of setting aside areas for industry, business, schools, apartments, residences and parks, all so located as not to interfere with one another.

The Planned City

Individuals plan years ahead for things they want to do. They plan trips, business enterprises, homes, farm developments, careers and many other things. So general is the idea of individual planning that a person who fails to plan for the future seems destined to failure.

But, in the case of communities and cities, until recent years the idea of planning was not common. In fact, a planned city was seldom heard of. The City of Washington, laid out by L'Enfant in the time of George Washington, is cited as an early example of city-planning; but even in this case the example is not altogether perfect, since the plan originally made was never accurately followed.

The idea of the planned city, however, is not new. Before the time of Christ, attempts were made in the cities of Egypt to lay out an orderly arrangement of streets with broad, tree-lined boulevards leading to the temples. Greece ornamented her streets with statuary, and Aristotle wrote of "one Hippodamus" as "a planner of cities." In mediaeval times, what plans were made were largely for immediate

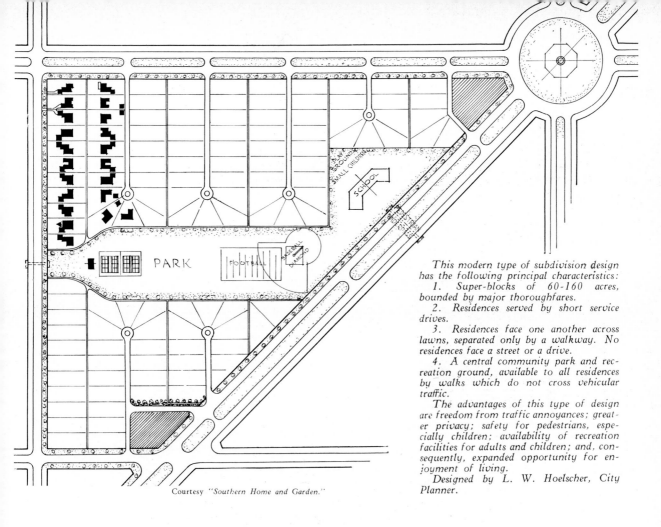

PARK
FOOTBALL
PLAY GROUND SMALL CHILDREN
SCHOOL
BRIDLE PATH

This modern type of subdivision design has the following principal characteristics:

1. Super-blocks of 60-160 acres, bounded by major thoroughfares.
2. Residences served by short service drives.
3. Residences face one another across lawns, separated only by a walkway. No residences face a street or a drive.
4. A central community park and recreation ground, available to all residences by walks which do not cross vehicular traffic.

The advantages of this type of design are freedom from traffic annoyances; greater privacy; safety for pedestrians, especially children; availability of recreation facilities for adults and children; and, consequently, expanded opportunity for enjoyment of living.

Designed by L. W. Hoelscher, City Planner.

Courtesy "Southern Home and Garden."

utility only, and almost at once outgrown. During the Renaissance, certain cities were built with the deliberate plan of "radial routes coördinated on geometric lines and reconciled at points of junction by circular or triangular parks." The military value of such an arrangement is obvious.

In America, we have allowed most of our cities just to grow up as did Topsy. Boston is a perfect example. There the cow-trails and paths of a few New England families determined the street system of old Boston, and the Boston of today is widely known for its winding, narrow streets, utterly inadequate for present day needs.

For many years we have realized that we should lay out our cities according to careful plans, so that property values may remain constant and transportation facilities adequate. We know this, but we do not do it. Congestion of population resulting partly from no ordinance against skyscrapers, slums with no parks or playgrounds, undesirable sections known as "blighted areas", valuable

Denver, Colorado, has one of the finest Civic Centers. Around this open area are its public buildings, such as its City and County Building, seen in this picture.

residence property ruined by lack of zoning—we have them all in both town and city. The high cost of distribution and the general high cost of city living are the result of the lack of broad, scientific city-planning.

The logical question to ask is, "If lack of city-planning is so unsatisfactory and so costly, why don't we do something about it? Why don't we begin to plan our towns and cities as we plan our lives?"

That would seem the right thing to do, but planning cities is

Courtesy "Parks and Recreation."

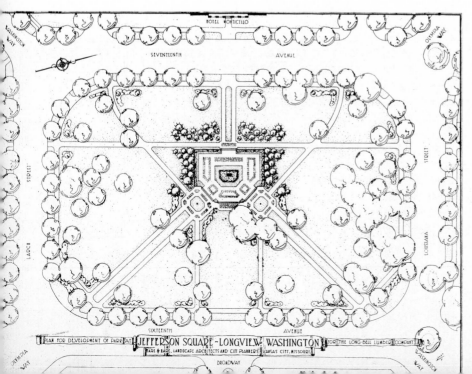

This is the plan for the Civic Center, Longview, Washington.

The entire city was designed before anyone lived in it. In fact, most of the streets were paved before people "moved in".

The idea of the 'Square' is not new. We have only to visit some of the old Mexican villages to see that hundreds of years ago people had the same desire to h a v e a central meeting-place, or a central court.

The firm of Hare & Hare, Kansas City, Missouri, were the Landscape Architects and City Planners.

Jefferson Square, Long-view, Washington, before development.

Courtesy "Parks and Recreation."

much more difficult than planning careers. The problems of civil engineering in connection with constructing streets and erecting buildings, securing drainage and providing power are very simple compared with the problems of human engineering, — that is, the problem of getting people of varied interests and ideas to agree upon a program of development. The influential citizen with property on the east side of the city will demand that the new highway pass by his land. Another person will block city improvements just because he cannot benefit directly and personally from such projects.

Courtesy "Parks and Recreation."

Jefferson Square, Long-view, Washington, after development.

Every home faces a park in Greenway Park Subdivision, Dallas, Texas. This affords ample play-areas and an opportunity for beautification. Children are not forced to cross streets to reach their playgrounds and the areas are sufficiently large to prevent too intensive use of any section.

The citizenship of every community should demand some similar scheme of residential development.

Courtesy "Southern Home and Garden."

Those communities that have done much in city-planning have found their greatest difficulty in the field of human engineering.

There are City Planners in this country, men who have studied city-plans and city-planning to find the best and most economical ways of correcting unsatisfactory city layouts and of planning new communities from the beginning so that their layout will remain satisfactory through all stages of the city's growth. They can save us costly mistakes if we will let them.

In every city, it is necessary to have factories, stores, filling-stations, homes, railroads and streets. If a city does not plan and zone its areas, these units are usually found all mixed together. For example, everyone has seen fine residential areas ruined by the erection of factories or filling-stations. Many citizens have saved for years to buy a home which, when paid for, is not worth what it cost because a store has been built next door. No one wants to live next door to a store or a factory. What the City Planner tries to do is to put into some orderly arrangement all these things which people must have in order to carry on the everyday affairs of their lives.

He designs a place for shops, a place for industries, a beautiful area for homes surrounded by parks and away from noise, a civic center for public buildings, and boulevards and parkways and safe highways for high speed traffic. If everyone were allowed to do as he pleases, such an orderly arrangement would be impossible. But by wisely planning the entire city, all these benefits can be secured for everyone. This is the reason that after a city is planned it is zoned, — that is, laws are enacted to compel people to abide by the plan. If a certain area is designed for residential purposes, our zoning laws will not permit stores to be built there. Zoning is the people's way of saying how property shall be used.

In some cities, zoning ordinances specify how tall the buildings are to be. In Los Angeles, for instance, the office-buildings in the business district may not be over twelve stories high. Such a provision is wise because tall buildings in cities place too many people on one spot. The congestion thus caused produces undesirable living conditions and makes traffic difficult. In New York City it has been figured that people lose a million dollars a day because of congestion. It costs more to transport articles from point to point within the city than it does to carry them nearly across the continent.

If we were to plan a model city, one of the first things to do would be to determine how large to allow the city to become. Most people would want it just as big as possible. That would be natural because of the advantages big cities afford. People never think of the disadvantages — great distances to travel, increased complexity of city government, unassimilated foreign quarters. Smaller cities need have none of the disadvantages of great cities, and can have nearly all the advantages. They can have fine schools, theaters, parks

This is the result of no zoning.

A modern apartment which has destroyed the landscape of a residential block and is sponging on t h e homes within i t s shadow for light and air, while cutting off these homes from their rightful share of Nature's gifts.

We cannot think of a beautiful city without beautiful buildings. Good architecture is an inspiration to good citizenship. This is a picture of the Masonic Temple in Fort Worth, Texas.

and beautiful buildings. American people are beginning to see this, and there is some indication that a decentralization process is taking place at the present time.

There is also a big disadvantage in living in a city that is too small to support fine stores, theaters, and other things that we all enjoy in larger cities. The Government has recently made a study which shows that communities under 9000 in population are undesirable except when close to other larger places. The hope is that industries can be moved to these small places so that more people

Today there is a tendency to remove many of the glaring signs and bill-boards from our streets.

Good taste displayed in a theater entrance where no portion of signs projects more than twelve inches beyond building-line.

can be supported. Perhaps the industry can be run during such time of the year when the citizens cannot work in the fields producing crops.

After we have determined the size of the city, we can design the street system to conform to the natural topography of the location. This is very important, if we are to avoid steep grades and to make the most of the possibilities nature has provided. We must determine where the business district should be. From this point the main streets should radiate, so that the business center will remain always in the same place. In some cities, where the streets form rectangles and there is no central point from which the main thoroughfares radiate, the center of the business area has moved several miles from its original location and property values have depreciated.

In designing our city, we will want a civic center to which we can point with pride. In this center we will build the city hall, library, auditorium, court-house and whatever other public buildings are needed. This is what the Greeks did with their Acropolis. In America, many cities have civic centers. Springfield, Massachusetts, has one, as have Denver, Cleveland, Los Angeles, San Francisco and many others.

A conglomeration of advertising features resulting only in confusion.

Courtesy "Texas Outlook."

Downtown plazas or courts are always pleasing and serve as a relief from the masonry and pavement. Burnett Park in Fort Worth, Texas, is here pictured.

In planning the residential areas of the city, we will arrange to have each house face a park or be near a playground. This is an essential feature in any city. It is natural for people with families to want a place for their children to play. In sections where there are no playgrounds, property values have decreased, because people have moved out into the newer sections where there is more room for their families.

Our city-plan must include a park system and park-drives. It is not enough that we have business streets and highways. We must take advantage of the natural beauty of our city by constructing park-drives to connect the parks located in all sections of the city. These drives will serve as a means of going from one part of town to another over avenues that are more attractive than the business streets and will lessen congestion on the downtown streets. Our city can be made a beautiful garden city. There is no reason why streets cannot be made beautiful, why our buildings cannot be examples of good architecture, why our whole environment cannot be made artistic. These are the things that attract new people to a city and make it grow.

A widely known example of a city planned from the beginning, after the fashion described here, is Canberra, the new Federal City of Australia, designed by Walter Burley Griffin. This city is located upon two hills and several valleys. The main avenue of the city connects the two hilltops and crosses the principal valley at right angles. This makes it possible for the streets which radiate from the various centers to interconnect in an interesting way. A good account of the plan of this city is given in the May, 1936, issue of the Geographic Magazine.

San Francisco built on a definite plan almost from the beginning, after her fire, as did Tokio after her earthquake.

The best known example of setting up a revamping plan and building towards it over a period of years is Chicago, with its transformed lake-front, its outer drive and its double-deck Wacker Drive. New York City also is trying to build itself over, with its George

(Photo, Courtesy Californians, Inc.).

Wide roadways, pedestrian walks, and lanes for horseback-riding in Golden State Park, San Francisco.

*The Landscape setting for the Buckingham Fountain in Grant Park, Chicago.
All of this land is man-made, being formerly covered by Lake Michigan.*

Washington and Triborough bridges, its tunnels and its elevated auto-roads to facilitate traffic, and its wholesome replacement of slums on the east side with park-ways and model tenements. Dallas and Fort Worth, Detroit and Cleveland, Oklahoma City and Tulsa all have a city-plan toward which they are working.

Longview, Washington, now a city of 10,000, was planned by the firm of Hare & Hare, Landscape Architects, of Kansas City, Missouri, and developed by the Long-Bell Lumber Company before there were any inhabitants. Today it is an excellent example of what can be accomplished by the application of modern principles of city-planning.

Every community, however small, should have a plan, and an attempt should be made to convince every citizen that the plan must be followed very closely. Everybody should be in favor of the plan and take an active interest in the building of his town or city. This idea of planning the place where we live is new to many people. It will require much talk on the advantages of such a scheme to change the viewpoint of some citizens. In fact, many of our towns and cities will not be planned and rebuilt until the students who are now in school have become active citizens. It is to them we look for assistance in the big problems of city-planning. It is theirs to carry on the ideal of "America, the Beautiful," with public parks for everyone's joy and well-planned communities which as long as they live shall continue to grow into greater beauty and efficiency.

The Story in Pictures

Our Wild Animal Friends

NATURE LOVER'S CREED

"I believe in Nature, and in God's out-of-doors.

I believe in pure air, fresh water, and abundant sunlight.

I believe in the mountains; and as I lift up mine eyes to behold them, I receive help and strength.

I believe that below their snowy crowns their mantles should be ever green.

I believe in the forests, where the sick may be healed and the weary strengthened; where the aged may renew their youth, and the young gather stores of wisdom which shall abide with them forever.

I believe that the groves were God's first temples, and that here all hearts should be glad, and no evil thought come to mar the peace.

I believe that all who seek shelter within these aisles should guard the noble heritage from harm, and the fire-fiend never be allowed to roam unwatched.

I believe in the highland springs and lakes, and would have noble trees stand guard around them; upon the mountain-sides I would spread a thick carpet of leaves and moss, through which the water might find its way into the valleys and onward to the ocean.

I believe in the giant trees which have stood for thousands of years, and pray that no harm shall come nigh them.

I believe in the axe of the *trained* woodsman, and would have it hew down the mature trees of today that we may secure lumber for our needs, and the trees of smaller growth have more light and air and space.

I believe in the seeds of the trees, and would gather and plant them; and I would care for the seedlings until they are ready to stand with their brothers in the forest and on the plains. Then the wilderness and the dry land shall be glad and the desert shall rejoice.

I believe in protecting the birds and the animals that live amidst the trees, and the ferns and mosses and blossoming plants.

I believe in all the beautiful things of Nature, and would preserve, protect, and cherish them."

"HOLLERIN' LIKE A LOON"

Photograph by Hobart V. Roberts, made at South Lake, New Yo
Courtesy "American Fores

HIS MAJESTY"—*The Brown Pelican in Florida.*

Photo by Sigfrid A. Larson. Courtesy *"American Forests."*

Feeding the Hippopotamus at the Philadelphia Zoo.

"WHAT'S THE USE"

Photograph by Lloyd Cooper, made in Sequoia National Park, California.

Courtesy *"American Forests."*

Grey squirrels appreciate t h e friendliness of man.

Mary L o u, o f Washington Park Zoological Society, Milwaukee, Wisconsin, looking through smoked glasses at the eclipse of the sun, August 31, 1932.

The snapping turtle is curious but not too friendly.

"Queen Tut" performing at the Fort Wort Zoo.

Feeding-time for the Sea Lions.

Courtesy *"Parks and Recreation."*

Courtesy *"Parks and Recreation."*

George P. Vierheller with a young Gorilla.

The photograph shows the popular director of the Zoological Garden at Forest Park, St. Louis, with a valuable young gorilla, brought to this country by J. L. Buck.

The Swamp in the vestibule of Steinhart Aquarium, San Francisco.

This contains alligators, crocodiles, turtles, fish, and frogs.

Courtesy "Parks and Recreation."

The Bewick Wren and her home.

Photograph by J. Carlton Van Duzer
Courtesy *Paul Riis.*

*The long-necked Giraffe
at the Philadelphia Zoo.*

Courtesy *Philadelphia Zoo*

Photograph by Canadian National Park Service.
Courtesy *Paul Riis.*

Deer in Velvet

Courtesy Los Angeles Park Department.

The Los Angeles Park Department has given these Elks a fine home.

A group of Polar Bears in the terrace set aside for them, San Antonio Zoo.

Courtesy "Parks and Recreation."

From the top of their mountain the Baboons at the Detroit Zoo have a fine chance to see the other animals.

A portion of Monkey Island or "Primate Paradise," showing one of the swimming-pools and, at the left, entrance to the cave which conceals the monkey-house, San Antonio Zoo.

Getting a thrill from the lions at close range—Outdoor lion grotto, at the Detroit Zoo.

A pack of polar panhandlers at the Detroit Zoo.

Courtesy "Parks and Recreation."

The Octopus at Steinhart Aquarium, San Francisco.

Antelope House, St. Louis Zoo, after completion. (View shows Chapman zebras in giraffe section before latter arrived. Note excellence of rock imitation in comparing with view of natural formation.)

Courtesy "Parks and Recreation."

When heavy snows come
the keeper broadcasts food.

Squirrels and Jays partaking of the furnished food.

Bison feeding in the Denver Mountain Parks Game Preserve.

Elk herd in the Denver Mountain Parks game preserve.

Bird Identification Case, along the Nature Trail.

The Reptile House at the Cincinnati Zoo.

SNOWTIME AT LAKE TAHOE, CALIFORNIA

*"Jingle, jingle, clear the way,
'Tis the merry, merry sleigh!"*

—G. W. PETTEE.

Recreation—the Ways of Leisure

TODAY man finds himself completely surrounded by his own works. Our great industrial age has developed at such a rapid rate that we hardly have had time to realize what we have been doing or even what we really wanted to do. We have thought only of machines, and more and more machines, until there has come a time when there are so many of them, so much pavement and so many buildings, row on row, that many thousands of our people are crowded into dark tenements where there is little sunshine and where there are few green lawns on which to play. Such a condition has resulted in poor health and a degraded citizenship for many of these thousands.

There have developed many problems with this great industrial growth of ours,—problems of how to handle traffic, and how best to house our people; problems of economics and of government. But one of the greatest is the problem of recreation. As people have increasing leisure time, the question of what to do with this leisure becomes more and more important.

The pictures which follow will give some idea of the way in which many cities have been and are solving this problem by creating efficiently organized recreation departments and by providing open areas for sunshine and for good wholesome play.

Courtesy "Parks and Recreation"

Hockey at night on the Union College hockey-rink, Schenectady, New York.

Courtesy "Parks and Recreation."

Toboggan-slide, Lynn Woods, Lynn, Massachusetts, illuminated for night recreation.

*Winter Sports Week —
Skating Derby at Lake of
the Isles, Minneapolis.*

*A Daring Jump. Alf
Engen establishing record
of 257 feet at Los Angeles
County Big Pine Recrea-
tion Camp.*

Happy days on the hills of Columbia Park, Minneapolis.

Ice-boating—Lake Cal-houn, Minneapolis.

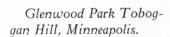

Glenwood Park Tobog-gan Hill, Minneapolis.

Interstate Ski Jumping Championship, Bear Mt. Park, Jan. 18, 1931.

I earnestly hope that in each of our local communities men and women interested in the public welfare will give increasing thought and time to this great democratic method of providing recreation for all the people, untrammeled by any motive except that of living fully and richly.

— FRANKLIN D. ROOSEVELT.

Toboggan-slides in the Palisades Interstate Park.

Courtesy *"Parks and Recreation."*

Skating in park swimming pool, Allegheny County Park, Pennsylvania.

Photograph by Paul Riis.

"Enrichment of Life"

TIME is the raw material out of which life is carved. Leisure is our own time. We ourselves are the employers of leisure. The shape or pattern of life often becomes largely a matter of how we use what is loosely called "spare time."

As far as accomplishment is concerned for millions of people, the day is done when the whistle blows. "Nothing to do until tomorrow" is the slogan. Aimless recreation follows. Yet, most of these people have vague ambitions of one sort or another. The time when these ambitions might be set in motion is the leisure time. By ignoring this use of leisure the best in life is tossed aside like an old newspaper. Such waste of time might be more readily justified if it led to contentment. On the contrary, no one is more bored with himself or leads a duller existence than the person who has no program for his after-working hours.

Most people do not use time with a purpose. They drift with it. Instead of making life, they permit it to happen. Their conversation is of yesterday and their thoughts of tomorrow. Many of the ancients were wiser. *"Carpe diem,"* meaning "Seize the day," was the advice of Horace two thousand years ago. "Make the most of today" is the sense of this expression. Forget yesterday, for yesterday is gone. Dismiss tomorrow. Tomorrow is never here. Live today! Grasp the fleeting moment by the forelock and use it now. Let it slip by and it is out of your grasp forever.

Above the timberline on Mount Hood. Here the people have become "winter sports conscious"—Olympic tryouts have been held, and 40,000 skiers have assembled to watch them.

Courtesy "American For

Courtesy "American Forests."

On the ski trail, in the Mount Hood National Forest. There are few, if any, great playgrounds in this country so ideally situated now for winter sports as Mount Hood—where for over a century few snowshoers were known and fewer skiers.

Time is the element out of which life is carved. I am thinking of the marble out of which sculptors carve their works of art. In a sense each of us is a sculptor. Day by day we hammer away at the marble which is time. Chip by chip it falls at our feet. The outline of a statue first appears rough, almost formless. Indeed, it is never wholly finished. To the last hour we apply the chisel. At length the hand relaxes and life is done. The statue is our life's work. It is the result of what we have done with time. If we have lived beautifully, it is beautiful. If we have lived usefully, the marble figure has, at least, a semblance of beauty. If we have lived badly, aimlessly, carelessly, our handiwork reflects the misuse of the primal material given us—Time.

JAMES A. MOYER,

Courtesy "Recreation."

Division of University Extension, Massachusetts Department of Education.

Dog Derby at Lake of the Isles, Minneapolis.

The Minnehikers on a winter day at Lake Harriet, Minneapolis.

Ski-jumping at Glenwood Park, Minneapolis.

*A friendly wind, a billowing
sail, and no speed regulations —
Lake Calhoun, Minneapolis.*

*Snow-modeling by Duluth,
Minnesota, school children.*

American Legion party climbing Mt. Hood, July 4, 1934.

Public bathing-beach, New Haven, Connecticut, May, 1933.

Courtesy "Parks and Recreation."

Great sport in a Nashville, Tennessee, pool.

Outdoor showers in wading-pool on a Milwaukee, Wisconsin, playground.

Courtesy "Parks and Recreation."

Blackfeet Indians with their tepees at Minnehaha Park, Minneapolis, Minnesota.

A close-up view of the Natatorium at Audubon Park, New Orleans, Louisiana.

Start of an Easter egg hunt, Logan Park Field-House, Minneapolis.

Teddy bears at the Lyndale Park pageant, Minneapolis.

Bath and field-house, showing part of the swimming pool (130 ft. by 400 ft.), Tibbetts Brook Park, Yonkers, New York, Westchester County Park System.

Gilmore D. Clarke, Landscape Architect; O. J. Gette, Consulting Architect; Hermann W. Merkel, General Superintendent.

Courtesy "Parks and Recreation."

The joys of t
bathing-beach

Courtesy Westchester County Park Commission.

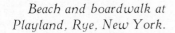

Beach and boardwalk at Playland, Rye, New York.

Members of Harry James' Trailfinders Boys' School on hike in Big Pines, Los Angeles County playground.

Recreation Service in Los Angeles County Mountain area.

Campfire scene—Indian ight at Big Pines Recrea-on Camp.

Recreation Service in Los ngeles County Mountain ea.

Kaymo electric motor-boats, Westlake Park, Los Angeles.

Courtesy "Parks and Recreation."

City Park trout fishing — an innovation in recreation — Salt Lake City Park.

Boy Scouts camping on the North Commons, Minneapolis.

Courtesy *Minneapolis Park Department.*

A Pushmobile Derby

Courtesy Minneapolis Park Department.

A Community Sing at Powderhorn Lake Park, Minneapolis.

Courtesy Minneapolis Park Department.

Courtesy Minneapolis Park Department.

"Scooter Race" on Nicollet Field Concrete Tennis Courts, Minneapolis.

Courtesy "Parks and Recreation."

The Olympic Games of 1932. Stella Walsh competing for Poland in the discus. She won the 300 meter dash. V. K. Brown, Director of Recreation in Chicago, in background.

Courtesy *"Parks and Recreation."*

The Olympic Games of 1932. Van Osdel, United States, and McNaughton, Canada, second and first place high jump winners.

Come, hoist the sail, the fast let go!
They're seated side by side;
Wave chases wave in pleasant flow;
The bay is fair and wide.

RICHARD HENRY DANA.

Sail Boating, Lake Calhoun, Minneapolis.

Courtesy *Minneapolis Park Department.*

Swans Guarding Their Young at Loring Park, Minneapolis.

Motor Sailboat Contest, Commons Wading-Pool, Minneapolis.

The Pet Show

Water lilies from the Pageant at Lyndale
Park, Minneapolis.

Courtesy *Minneapolis Park Department.*

Walking the Beam.

Courtesy *Minneapolis Park Department.*

Just a Game of Horseshoe.

Bubble Time.

Story Time in Powderhorn Park, Minneapolis.

The Fairy Queen in the Pageant at Lyndale Park, Minneapolis.

One of the five illuminated Ball Diamonds, where one thousand business men play weekly, with over thirty-five thousand spectators.—Miami, Florida.

*Sunset on Lake Calhoun,
Minneapolis.*

Lake of the Isles, Kennilworth Lagoon, Minneapolis.

...dle Trails in Griffith ...k, Los Angeles, Cali-...nia.

Courtesy Los Angeles Park Department.

Old Timers Play on Huge Outdoor Checkerboard, Oak Park, Illinois. The first game being played on Oak Park's new big public checkerboard. L. Harbin, 80 years old, and Louis A. Schaukel, 77, waged the contest, with a new hat offered by Mayor Feeley as the prize.

Courtesy "Parks and Recreation."

Van Cleve Park Shelter House and Pool, Minneapolis, Minnesota.

Lake Louise and Mt. Whyte, Banff National Park, Alberta, Canada.

An old game revived—the Archery Club, Fort Worth, Texas.

Above—Fishing from the pier at Huntington Park.

Left—Nature group at the Bedford Reservation.

*A rugged shoreline, the sound of waves over
rock and a glistening reflection of sunshine.*

*Lake Worth, Fort Worth, Texas, not only serves as a water supply for the
city but also as a recreation center. The C. C. C. boys have built roads and
hiking trails along the shoreline and have constructed beautiful shelter houses
for picnicking.*

Landscape Architecture

"By their works you shall know them." Such a statement is generally true of professional men and women. We know an architect by the buildings he designs; an engineer, by the bridges he may build. But do we really know by his works just who is a landscape architect? I am afraid we do not, because a truly great landscape architect designs so many things that aren't supposed to be known as man-made creations. So often the landscape effect, to be successful, must be natural; and appearing natural, we give nature, alone, credit, forgetting that somewhere behind the scenes there was a human being of vision who had caught the spirit of the natural, and who possessed enough genius to leave us all unaware that the hand of man had played any part in the resulting beauty surrounding us.

The field of landscape architecture is most comprehensive. It may have as its problem the designing of a formal private garden or the creation of a gigantic city plan that will affect the lives of every individual within that city. In brief, the landscape architect has to do with land design, changing the topography, constructing roads and walks, — creating lawns and wooded areas, all in such a way as to make our environment more useful as well as more beautiful.

Contributing to the success of the landscape architect is a general understanding of horticulture, agriculture, geology, forestry, engineering, social engineering, economics and art. No other profession demands so broad a knowledge as does this new and fascinating field of Landscape Architecture.

The pictures that follow illustrate the wide range of work of landscape architects and of those in closely allied fields of endeavor.

Sculpture, a fine art sister of Landscape Architecture, is doing much to carry on the spirit of many of our great citizens as well as to decorate our parks with great works of art.

A close-up of the Washington Head taken a few days before the unveiling.

(Rushmore Memorial, Black Hills, South Dakota.)

Courtesy "Parks and Recreation."

"In his arms he bore a maiden." — Minnehaha and Hiawatha Bronze Statue. Minnehaha Park, Minneapolis, Minnesota.

Courtesy "Parks and Recreation."

Rushmore Project Model partially carved.

(Insert). Gutzon Borglum, the Sculptor.

The City Hall at Pasadena, California, is an inspiration to its entire citizenship. It would be well if all our public buildings were examples of good architecture.

The main entrance to San Antonio's million and a quarter dollar school plant, — Thomas Jefferson High School.

The landscaping of the grounds at William James Junior High School, Fort Worth, Texas, has added dignity to this institution of learning and is a source of inspiration to the students and to the entire neighborhood.

Rose Garden at Exposition Park, Los Angeles, containing 15,793 rose bushes.   This is one of the largest rose gardens in America.

An airplane view of Lake of the Isles, with Cedar Lake in the background. This lake property is used as one of the city's parks and is controlled by the Park Department.

Great Falls from Virginia side, near Washington, D. C.

Courtesy "Texas Outlook."

The celebration of the Texas Centennial, 1936, was responsible for the creation of a new and beautiful park for the people of Dallas, Texas. The grounds will be used as a permanent park and for the annual State Fair.

Photograph by R. C. M.

Courtesy "Southern Home and Garden."

The people of Dallas, Texas, have been wise in following the suggestions of George Kessler—City Planner—in preserving the natural beauty of Turtle Creek, as this is now one of the most beautiful residential sections in America.

A modern chalet is provided in Glenwood Park by the Minneapolis Park Department.

St. Petersburg's Recreation Pier (Florida).

This is the largest recreation pier in the South. Built at a cost of a million dollars, it provides a ballroom, assembly room, studio of radio station W. S. V. N., a steamship office, bait house, eighteen fishing balconies, and parking space for 1200 automobiles.

Mushing along through Glenwood Park,
Minneapolis, Minnesota.

Courtesy Minneapolis Park Department.

Courtesy *"Parks and Recreation."*

Japanese plum-trees in
bloom on a Victoria boul-
evard in February.

(Courtesy George I. Warren, Commissioner Victoria and Island Publicity
Bureau, — Canada.)

THE BRONX RIVER PARK-
WAY is a masterpiece of landscape
architecture. The roadway is an
example of gracefulness of curve
and profile. The structures, such
as guard-rails and directional signs,
are in keeping with the beauty of
the wooded areas. All planting
adds to the enjoyment of the native growth rather than detracts
from our feeling that this is truly
rural. This great parkway, extend-
ing from New York City to Bear
Mountain, is one of the worthwhile things to see when traveling
in the East.

The picture is of the Bronx
Parkway Extension — Valhalla,
New York.

All buildings such as filling-stations and taverns are carefully designed. This is a gasoline-station
and Woodland Lake Tavern.

Gasoline filling-station, Hutchinson River Parkway, Westchester County, New York.

Gasoline pumps are hidden in well-house.

Bridges ought to have the self-same qualifications we judge necessary in all other buildings, which are that they should be commodious, beautiful, a n d lasting.

—Andrea Palladio, 1518-1580.

Kitchawan Bridge over Croton Lake Crossing of Bronx Parkway Extension.

Courtesy "Parks and Recreation.

The bridges along the Bronx River Parkway are all unusual as well as very beautiful.
Bridge over Hutchinson River Parkway at Mill Road, New Rochelle, New York.
(Gilmore D. Clarke, Landscape Architect; A. G. Hayden, Designing Engineer).

Woodlands Lake Tavern Restaurant and Gasoline Station on Saw Mill
River Parkway in Everit W. Macy Park.

Courtesy "Parks and Recreation."

Briarcliff Wells Gasoline and Concession Building — Bronx Parkway Extension.

(Clinton F. Lloyd—Architectural Designer).

Courtesy *"Parks and Recreation."*

Courtesy Westchester County Park Commission.

THE CREED OF THE OPEN ROAD

The beauty of the open road is not policed, except by the honor of the traveler.

I, therefore, who love the freedom of the open road shall not permit that freedom to degenerate into license.

Capable of perceiving the beauty of trees, I shall be incapable of destroying that beauty for those who may follow.

The living radiance of the flowers brightens my journey. I shall not wantonly wrest from them that life and radiance.

It is the very order and cleanliness of a wayside camp that tempts me to halt for rest. I shall not, then, be so boorish a guest as to leave it in disorder and uncleanliness.

I shall respect the lives, the property and the customs of the community through which I pass, and thus endeavor to leave agreeable recollections of the motor and the motorist.

Privilege entails obligation.

I, who ride the open road, value and enjoy its countless privileges.

Equally, therefore, do I assume —with good will and sincerity— its few and legitimate obligations.

—American Automobile Association.

Bronx River Parkways, Scarsdale, New York.

Hutchinson River Par[k]way, Westchester Count[y] New York.

(Reinforced concrete rigid fra[me] bridge over the Parkway at Mt. Vern[on] New York. Drive is planned for fut[ure] widening to 60 feet. Forty feet [of] pavement in place in four 10 f[oot] lanes).

(Gilmore D. Clarke, Landscape Ar[ch]itect; A. G. Hayden, Designing [En]gineer).

Courtesy *"Parks and Recreation."*

Courtesy Westchester County Park Commission.

Pines Bridge Road on Bronx River Parkway Extension.

Courtesy *"Parks and Recreation."*

Farragut Gasoline and Police Station—Saw Mill River Parkway, Yonkers, New York.

(Clinton F. Lloyd, Architectural De-signer).

Mount Vernon Memorial Highway.
Completed pavement approaching Mount Vernon, prior to landscaping.

A part of the automobile parking-area of the Mount Vernon terminus of the Mount Vernon Memorial Highway, after completion of landscaping, just prior to being placed in use.

THE FORT WORTH BOTANIC GARDEN

This Garden, designed by the firm of Hare & Hare of Kansas City, Missouri, provides the people of Fort Worth, Texas, not only a rare beauty spot but also an opportunity to study all the plants that will grow in this section. It is an outdoor library of living plants.

This is the artist's drawing of the Garden made before the development was started.

The relief workers begin work on the Garden, changing a mud hole into a thing of beauty.

Just a year after work began, there stands a Garden, which is a monument to the heroic victims of the depression, for it was these men who toiled that beauty might be created.

Photo by R. C. M. for Fort Worth Park Department.

The Fort Worth Botanic Garden is not only an outstanding example of work accomplished through the various Federal work relief programs, but it is also a demonstration of what can be done where people have plans and dreams of making their city more beautiful and abundant in recreation facilities. Cities without plans wasted much of their relief labor during the past four years.

Fort Worth's Botanic Garden has achieved wide-spread fame from the thousands of visitors who see it each year. As many as 18,000 people have visited the Garden in a single day.

Dominating this outdoor library of living plants is the Rose Garden with its 10,000 rose bushes, its intricate pattern of rose beds, and its graceful trellises.

Courtesy *"Texas Outlook."*

Above is the shelter house at the main entrance of the Garden, seen across the lake which serves as a reflecting basin, and the landscaped terrace.

Natural springs in the Botanic Garden supply water for a series of lakes. Rustic bridges, lagoons and waterfalls add much to the beauty of the garden, and the lakes afford a splendid opportunity for the cultivation of water plants.

Nature trails wind through the heavily wooded area where every tree and shrub is marked for study. Rustic benches are provided at frequent intervals along the trail so that one need not tire.

The azure of the sky and the green of trees reflected in water.
Fort Worth Botanic Garden.

Photo by R. C. M. for Fort Worth Park Department.   Courtesy "Southern Home and Garden."

Beauty is all about us every day, everywhere, if we have the eye to see it and the mind to recognize it and enjoy it. We have it in all the great outdoors: we can see it in the flash of a blue jay's wing, in the shapes of the clouds as they float endlessly on in the glorious sky. We can see it in the lines of the meandering stream and in the curves of far distant hills. We can see it in the design and color of the simplest flower at the roadside.

—ELIZABETH W. ROBERTSON.

The Reflecting Pool, Fort Worth Botanic Garden.

Willows along the shore of Lake Worth — Fort Worth, Texas.

Courtesy *"Texas Outlook."*

Sail Boating on Eagle Mountain Lake, Fort Worth, Texas.

Hiking trail along Lake Worth—built by C. C. C.

Photo by R. C. M.

The Bridle Path, Akron, Ohio, Metropolitan Park System

The citizens of Houston, Texas, will always be reminded of its romantic history by this inspiring statue of Sam Houston, placed at the entrance to Hermann Park.

The development of the Park System of Houston. Texas. has kept pace with that city's most re-markable industrial growth. Here the citizens have constructed Hermann Park Golf Course on a tract of land covered with beautiful pine-trees. The lower picture shows the entrance to Hermann Park.

One of the most beautiful natural parks in the South is Cameron Park, Waco, Texas. Here the beauty of the bluffs and of the trees along the Brazos River will be preserved forever for the enjoyment of all the people.

Along the roadway unmarred by billboards and shacks.

This is a reproduction of one of 780 photographs submitted by Kodak employees all over the world in the Ninth Annual Kodak International Salon of Photography, held in Rochester, New York.

"Too close life crowds.
There is no place to hide.
From feverish days my heart throbs in
    my side, —
'Let us take time, take time.'
Let us take time to know the thoughts
    of men;
Time to know beauty; and time to feel
    again
Calm and content of soul — the quiet
    power
Of meditation through a gentle hour;
Time for the book, the song, the golden
    weather
Made for the happiness of friends to-
    gether;
Time to *believe*; and time to lift the bars
'Twixt us and truth, 'twixt heart-beat
    and the stars,
Before our breath is spent, before life's
    mill
Grinds all too fine.
Let us this hour be still,
Let us take time — take time."

Steps in Washington Park, St. Joseph, Missouri.

Courtesy *"Parks and Recreation."*

Our appreciation of water in the landscape depends to a great degree upon the marginal treatment of the land. The combined embankment, promenade, and overhanging cherry-trees in Potomac Park, Washington, add to the picture of the tidal reservoir.

Scenes from Our National Capital

The Lincoln Memorial Reflecting Pool in West Potomac Park as it appears today, looking east.

The Mall from the United States Capitol, as it appeared February 28, 1936.

Courtesy *"Parks and Recreation."*

Japanese cherry-trees in West Potomac Park, Washington, D. C.

Courtesy *"Parks and Recreation."*

The Bandstand, Forest Park, St. Louis.

Bowling on the Green at the Miami, Florida, Club House.

Park Planning by Aerial Survey.

Aerial map of Sharon Woods taken in October, 1931, before the land was purchased. This is one of the thousand pictures taken to form the survey of Hamilton County, Ohio.

An oblique aerial view of Sharon Woods, Hamilton County, Ohio, taken in February, 1933, showing the roads and bridge that have been constructed, and the cornfields sown to permanent grass.

*The California Fan Pa
u s e d in street planti
about the State Capi
grounds has much d
nity.*

*Palm Walk. South Park,
Los Angeles.*

*Lagoons in Eneine Par
Los Angeles, Californ*

Municipal Rose Garden at Elizabeth Park, Hartford, Connecticut.

Photo by Prawitz Studios.
Courtesy "Parks and Recreation."

The autumn colors are gorgeous—the elms a golden mass.
A St. Joseph, Missouri, Park Drive.

The Art Museum in
Volunteer Park,
Seattle, Washington.

. Rhododendrons in
Volunteer Park,
Seattle, Washington.

Lake Harriet, Minneapolis.

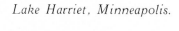

Minnehaha Falls, Minneapolis.

Lilacs in Lyndale Park, Minneapolis, Minnesota.

Twilight in Mohawk Park, Tulsa, Oklahoma.

Bolleana Poplars, Lake of Isles, Minneapolis, Minnesota.

Courtesy Minneapolis Park Department.

Mississippi Park, Minneapolis, Minnesota.

Courtesy *Minneapolis Park Department.*

The Crimson Ramblers at the Rose Garden, Lyndale Park, Minneapolis, Minnesota.

"There is no strength to the life which has no quiet moments."

Schmitz Park, Seattle, Washington.

Courtesy *"Parks and Recreation."*

The McDonogh Oak—One of New Orleans' Duelling Oaks.
It is 500 years old. The spread of branches is 136 feet. Every city should protect its old, historic trees.

Rhododendrons of San Francisco's Golden Gate Park. The beauty of this park is entirely man-made, as it was once a great stretch of sand.

Courtesy *"Parks and Recreation."*

A commanding point in a city is an asset on any occasion, but especially so in the case of Telegraph Hill, San Francisco, which rises above vast stretches of water.

Courtesy "Parks and Recreation."

Courtesy "Parks and Recreation."

Silent Night—St. Joseph, Missouri, Park.

Cherry-blossoms in the Japanese Tea Garden at Golden Gate Park, San
Francisco.

Section of Woodward Park Rock Gardens, Tulsa, Oklahoma.

Scene in Riverside Park, Wichita, Kansas.

"The Park Executive has his greatest opportunity for city beautification in the public parks of his city."

Rapids above Cumberland Falls, Kentucky.

(The water drops 12 feet in the last 200 yards above the brink. Giant trees of finest verdure guard either bank of the river.)

Courtesy "Parks and Recreation."

The ceaseless play of light, color and sound of a waterfall are always a source of human interest in the landscape. A scene in a California Botanical Garden.

"Have you ever been to Texas in the Spring?" — *Bluebonnets paint the hillsides blue.*

Bridle path in Audubon Park, New Orleans.

Courtesy "Parks and Recreation."

The value of street planting is evident in cases like the above, where trees form a glorious vista.

Mesquite Tracery.

The Orchid.

A-riding we will go! The Bridle Trail, Trinity Park, Fort Worth, Texas.

Shaded Waters.

Courtesy "Parks and Recreation."

Top of Giant's Steps, Banff National Park, Alberta, Canada.

Mt. Assiniboine and Lake Magog, Banff National Park, Alberta, Canada.

Lake Louise, Banff National Park, Alberta, Canada.

OUT IN THE FIELDS WITH GOD.

The little cares that fretted me,
  I lost them yesterday
Among the fields, above the sea,
  Among the winds at play,
Among the lowing of the herds,
  The rustling of the trees,
Among the singing of the birds,
  The humming of the bees.
The foolish fears of what might happen,
  I cast them all away,
Among the clover-scented grass,
  Among the new-mown hay,
Among the husking of the corn,
  Where drowsy poppies nod,
Where ill thoughts die and good are
    born,—
  Out in the fields with God.

    —ELIZABETH BARRETT BROWNING.

BACK FROM THE MOUNTAINS.

I have come back from the mountains,
  Back from the snow-white peaks;
Back from the crimson sunsets
  With opal and golden streaks.

Back from the glacial torrents,
  Tumultuous mad moraines;
Back from the creviced canyons
  And wandering refrains.

Back——but I'm bringing with me
  Vision and song and scent;
Visions of glacial canyons
  With glorified colors blent;

Hymns in the darkness soughing
  Through canyons of infinite time;
Thunder and tumbling rivers,
  Brooks and the winds sublime.

Highways of high horizons
  Forever my feet have trod—
For I have come back from the mountains
  And tramping the trails with God.

　　　　　　—WILLIAM L. STIDGER.

Courtesy "Parks and Recreation."

At the edge of Nisqually Glacier, showing the south side of the Mountain, Rainier National Park.

Jefferson Park Primitive Area —north side of Mt. Jefferson, Oregon.

The cool depths of this ever-green forest and the towering majesty of "The Mountain That Was God" are typical of the beauties and the wonders that make the Pacific Northwest a "Land Set Apart."

Courtesy *"Texas Outlook."*

Of all man's work of art a cathedral is the greatest. A vast and majestic tree is greater than that.
—Henry Ward Beecher.

Rock and Water Do a Picture Make.

Along the Rio Grande, where the Federal Government hopes to create the Big Bend International Park.

Cascades at Buttermilk Falls State Park, south of Ithaca, New York.

Lucifer Falls, Enfield Glen State Park, near Ithaca, New York.

It is noble when a man lays out gardens, levels terraces and plants woods for no other benefit than for his successors.

—George Buchanan, in "Passage Through the Present".

CONCLUSION

To you who have read this book, we can only say:

1. Love the outdoors and live in it.

2. Love beauty and learn to create it.

3. Think in terms of others: "What have I to enjoy that every-one also might have?"

4. Become a citizen fit to live where beauty dwells and where men are free—free to contribute something of good to the welfare of all.

Photograph by Paul Riis

NATIONAL MONUMENTS

National Monuments	Location	Area (acres)	Special Characteristics
Devil's Tower	Wyoming	1,152	Remarkable natural rock tower, of volcanic origin, 1,200 feet in height.
Montezuma Castle	Arizona	160 (Estimated)	Prehistoric cliff-dweller ruin of unusual size, situated in a niche in face of a vertical cliff. Of scenic and ethnologic interest.
El Morro	New Mexico	240	Enormous sandstone rock eroded in form of a castle, upon which inscriptions had been placed by early Spanish explorers. Contains cliff-dweller ruins. Of great historic, scenic and ethnologic interest.
Petrified Forest	Arizona	25,625	Abundance of petrified coniferous trees, one of which forms a small natural bridge. Is of great scientific interest.
Chaco Canyon	New Mexico	20,629 (Estimated)	Numerous cliff-dweller ruins, including communal houses, in good condition. Considerable excavation done at several of the ruins.
Muir Woods (Donated to the U. S.)	California	426.43	One of the most noted redwood groves in California. Was donated by Hon. William Kent, ex-Member of Congress. Located 7 miles from San Francisco.
Pinnacles	California	2,980.26	Many spirelike rock formations, 600 to 1,000 feet high, visible many miles; also numerous caves and other formations.
Natural Bridges	Utah	2,740 (Estimated)	3 natural bridges, among the largest examples of their kind. Largest bridge is 222 feet high, 65 feet thick at top of arch; arch is 128 feet wide; span, 261 feet; height of span, 157 feet. Other two slightly smaller.
Lewis & Clark Cavern (Donated to the U. S.)	Montana	160	Immense limestone cavern of great scientific interest, magnificently decorated with stalactite formations. Now closed to the public because of depredations by vandals.
Tumacacori	Arizona	10	Ruins of Franciscan mission dating from 17th century. Being restored by National Park Service as rapidly as funds permit.
Navajo	Arizona	360 (Estimated)	Numerous pueblo, or cliff-dweller, ruins in good preservation.
Shoshone Cavern	Wyoming	210	Cavern of considerable extent, near Cody.
Gran Quivira	New Mexico	560 (Estimated)	One of the most important of earliest Spanish mission ruins in the Southwest. Monument also contains pueblo ruins.
Sitka	Alaska	57 (Estimated)	Park of great natural beauty and historic interest as the scene of massacre of Russians by Indians. Contains 16 totem poles of best native workmanship.
Rainbow Bridge	Utah	160	Unique natural bridge of great scientific interest and symmetry. Height 309 feet above water, and span is 278 feet, in shape of rainbow.
Colorado	Colorado	13,883	Contains many lofty monoliths and is wonderful example of erosion. Of great scenic beauty and interest.
Papago Saguaro	Arizona	1,940.43	Splendid collection of characteristic desert flora and numerous pictographs. Interesting rock formations.
Dinosaur	Utah	80	Deposit of fossil remains of prehistoric animal life of great scientific interest.
Capulin Mountain	New Mexico	681	Cinder cone of geologically recent formation.
Verendrye	North Dakota	253.04	Includes Crowhigh Butte, peculiar mountain formation, from which Explorer Verendrye first beheld territory beyond the Missouri River.
Casa Grande From 6/22/1892 until 8/3/1918, classified as a National Park	Arizona	472.5	These ruins are one of the most noteworthy relics of a prehistoric age and people within the limits of the United States. Discovered in ruinous condition in 1694.
Katmai	Alaska	1,087,990 (Estimated)	Wonderland of great scientific interest in the study of volcanism. Phenomena exist upon a scale of great magnitude. Includes "Valley of Ten Thousand Smokes".
Scotts Bluff	Nebraska	1,893.83	Region of historic and scientific interest. Many famous old trails traversed by the early pioneers in the winning of the West, passed over and through this Monument.
Yucca House (Donated to the U. S.)	Colorado	9.6	Located on eastern slope of Sleeping Ute Mountain. Ruins of great archaeological value, relic of prehistoric inhabitants.
Fossil Cycad	South Dakota	320	Area containing deposits of plant fossils.
Aztec Ruin (Donated to the U. S.)	New Mexico	4.6	Prehistoric ruin of pueblo type containing 500 rooms.

NATIONAL MONUMENTS (Continued)

National Monuments	Location	Area (acres)	Special Characteristics
Hovenweep	Utah — Colorado	285.8	Four groups of prehistoric towers, pueblos, and cliff-dwellings.
Pipe Spring	Arizona	40	Old stone fort and spring of pure water in desert region serve as memorial to early western pioneer life.
Carlsbad Cave	New Mexico	719.22	Limestone caverns of extraordinary proportions and of unusual beauty.
Craters of the Moon	Idaho	24,960	Weird volcanic region containing remarkable fissure eruption, together with its associated volcanic cones, craters, lava flows, caves, natural bridges, and other phenomena.
Wupatki	Arizona	2,234.10	Prehistoric dwellings of ancestors of Hopi Indians.
Glacier Bay	Alaska	1,164,800	Contains tidewater glaciers of first rank.

NATIONAL PARKS

National Park and date	Location	Area in sq. miles	Distinctive Characteristics
Hot Springs 1832	Middle Arkansas	1-1/2	46 hot springs said to possess healing properties—Many hotels and boarding houses in adjacent city of Hot Springs—Bathhouses under public control.
Yellowstone 1872	Northwestern Wyoming	3,348	More geysers than in all rest of world together—Boiling springs—Mud volcanoes—Petrified forests—Grand Canyon of the Yellowstone, remarkable for gorgeous coloring—Large lakes and waterfalls—Wilderness inhabited by deer, elk, bison, moose, antelope, bear, mountain sheep, etc.
Yosemite 1890	Middle eastern California	1,125	Valley of world-famed beauty—Lofty cliffs—Romantic vistas—Waterfalls of extraordinary height—3 groves of big trees—Large areas of snowy peaks—Waterwheel falls.
Sequoia 1890	Middle eastern California	604	The Big Tree National Park—Scores of sequoia trees from 20 to 30 feet in diameter, thousands over 10 feet in diameter — Includes Mount Whitney, highest peak in continental United States.
General Grant 1890	Middle California	4	Created to preserve the celebrated General Grant Tree, 40.3 feet in diameter—6 miles from Sequoia National Park.
Mount Rainier 1899	West central Washington	325	Largest accessible single-peak glacier system—28 glaciers, some of large size—48 square miles of glacier, 50 to 1,000 feet thick—Remarkable subalpine wild-flower fields.
Crater Lake 1902	Southern Oregon	249	Lake of extraordinary blue in crater of extinct volcano, no visible inlet or outlet—Sides 1,000 feet high.
Platt 1902	Southern Oklahoma	1-1/3	Sulphur and other springs possessing curative properties—Under Government regulation.
Wind Cave 1903	South Dakota	17	Large natural cavern.
Sullys Hill 1904	North Dakota	1-1/5	Wooded hilly tract on Devils Lake.
Mesa Verde 1906	Southern Colorado	77	Most notable and best preserved prehistoric cliff dwellings in United States, if not in the world.
Glacier 1910	Northwestern Montana	1,534	Rugged mountain region of unsurpassed alpine character — 250 glacier-fed lakes of romantic beauty—60 small glaciers—Peaks of unusual shape—Precipices thousands of feet deep—Fine trout fishing.
Rocky Mountain 1915	Northern Colorado	378	Heart of the Rockies—Snowy Range, peaks 11,000 to 14,250 feet altitude—Remarkable records of glacial period.
Hawaii 1916	Hawaii	242	Two active volcanoes, Mauna Loa, largest in the world, and Kilauea, whose lake of bubbling lava is world famed—A third volcano, Haleakala, crater 8 miles wide.
Lassen Volcanic 1916	Northern California	124	Active volcano — Lassen Peak, 10,460 feet in altitude — Cinder Cone, 6,907 feet—Hot Springs—Mud geysers.
Mount McKinley 1917	South central Alaska	2,645	Highest mountain in North America—Rises higher above surrounding country than any mountain in the world.
Grand Canyon 1919	Northern Arizona	1,009	Greatest example of stream erosion in the world — More than 10 miles wide—more than 1 mile deep.
Lafayette 1919	Maine Coast	12	Group of granite mountains rising upon Mount Desert Island.
Zion 1919	Southwestern Utah	120	Magnificent gorge (Zion Canyon), depth from 1,500 to 2,500 feet, with precipitous walls, of great beauty and scenic interest.

3